# THE DARKENED CROWN

## GEORGINA MAKALANI

Also by Georgina Makalani

The Last Dragon Skin Chronicles:
The Empty Crown
The Lost Endeavour
Shadows Awaken

The Magics of Rei-Een:
The Hidden Princess
Hidden Promises
The Hidden Phoenix

The Raven Crown Series:
Raven's Dawn
The Caged Raven
Raven's Edge

The Legend of Iski Flare (Novella series):
The Legend Begins
Red Wolves
The Riddle of Daralis
The Last Child
The Tree Maiden
Reflections
The Beast
Circus of Wonders

Other Stories:
The Mark of Oldra
The Heart of Oldra

Short Stories:
Stuffed Frogs and Spinning Teacups
Searcher
The Silence (in Glimpses)
Short Stories:
Stuffed Frogs and Spinning Teacups
Searcher
The Silence (in Glimpses

# 1

Ana Merrin, Queen of Ilia and beyond, stood slowly from the stone throne. The soldier before her flinched. His thick sandy hair covered his face as he bowed low before her, and although he put his hand to his chest, it didn't touch the cool, dark metal of his breastplate, nor was there any respect behind it.

"Majesty," he whispered, his voice carrying through the empty space.

The long train of her forest-green dress dragged behind her as she stepped down to meet the man. She drank in the tension and fear ebbing from his still-bent form, sighing with the pleasure of it.

"There is no sign of him, Your Majesty."

She allowed her growl of disapproval to echo through the room. She appreciated it cooler, darker, and she'd had thick curtains installed to cover the large window that would otherwise illuminate the entire room.

"Majesty," he murmured.

"I will not have your human terms used in my presence. The boy might have been *your* majesty, but my title is more." Ana tried not to sigh. She had told herself it was habit and that they were doing what they thought would please her, but it grated on her very soul.

"So, not found then?" she prompted. He raised his head before dipping his gaze back to the ground.

"We have searched the capital."

"And beyond?"

The man slipped to his knees, and she allowed her sigh of

frustration to be heard. She had sent several of them to the beyond. They saw it as punishment, but it was a gift to her own. Either way, it had been enough to ensure those who remained did as they were told.

"The kingdom is much larger than the capital alone," she said.

"Majesty," he wheezed, his relief evident. She leaned over him, her long fingers pressed into his arm as she breathed into his ear, and his fear increased.

She drank it in, tempted for a moment to put her parched lips to his skin, but she restrained herself. She needed him to still function at some level so he could do as she required. "Captain Barlow," she hissed, too close. He failed to not flinch away from her. "Do you need some incentive?"

"Majesty?" he asked in return, and she could see every scared image that flashed through his mind.

"Major Barlow," she whispered, allowing her tongue to taste the fear on his skin. "Take men; send men out into the kingdom to find him."

He leapt to his feet, nodding wildly. "Is it only the boy you seek?"

She inclined her head. He wanted to ask why she didn't send her other soldiers out into the world—she could see it at the tip of his tongue—but he held it back. "Well done, Major. I knew I had selected the very best man for the job."

He bowed, his fist thumping loudly on his breastplate before he turned for the door.

"Major," she called after him.

He turned slowly, warily.

"Take one of the children with you."

"Majesty," he sighed, and the shadows followed him from the room.

Ana moved to the throne in a heartbeat, never tiring of using the shadows. Now that she had adjusted to this world, she rarely needed the other to nourish her. She sat back, running her long, dark nails over the hard, black stone of the armrest. They had remained so close in those first days when she had taken the crown—was handed the crown—and worked to subdue the people into accepting her.

It hadn't been very hard, not with her children encouraging the new way of life. She had felt the boy and the soldier, the little girl who glowed and even the sword master who thought too often of trying to hold her. And then they had gone. She had tried her best, but the bond between them appeared to be broken and she couldn't sense them like she had. She could have visited any part of the kingdom herself, and for a moment she had a longing to stand in the sea and feel the sand between her toes. It passed quickly.

*You cannot leave our throne.*

"I am well aware of what I can and can't do," she hissed at the voice inside her, the magic still trying to gain control. In many ways it had, but Ana was sure all it had done was show her to be the woman she was, the woman she had been all along. She had left the throne and the castle before, and no one had tried to take it back. No one would dare.

So many supported her. So many more of her shadows were settled in the world, most of which were unseen by the people unless she wanted them to be. They were useful in their own way, swaying the people, keeping the peace. Ana wondered what the regent had done for all those years.

The lords were encouraged to continue with their tribute. The world hadn't changed too much, only in gaining a queen when they had expected a king.

She huffed again at the idea of him, the boy who would have used her. But she had worked that well enough to her advantage. The world was hers, not his. And despite his want, he had not tried to take it back.

It was the little dragon and her father who worried Ana, not that she would admit such a thing to anyone—barely even to the magic inside her, although she knew it had a stronger hold on her than she wanted. Something had shifted in the girl once she had found her wings; something far stronger than Ana had expected to see had emerged, something that might have even surprised Endeavour.

For she wasn't all dragon, the little princess. But no matter what she was, she saw more of Ana and their future than Ana could herself. That frightened her. Scared her, for Ana had seen so much in the months since the crown had fitted snuggly onto her head. But she couldn't see them, despite knowing Salima saw her.

If only she had understood just what Salima was when she first came to the capital. Ana had seen an ally in the girl in many ways, despite only using her to get to Ed, and the girl had been sad when she had shared Ana's dreams.

Ana stood slowly now, wondering if she had somehow given the girl all she needed to be the strong little dragon she was. Or was she something bigger now? She had been more than a child when Ana had seen her at the shop where Ed had rallied the people. She had seen a princess. And she should have disposed of her then, but she hadn't fully understood the threat Salima would become.

Ana had sent the children out to scour the lands, seek out their heat, but they had returned with no news. And yet, deep within herself, Ana knew just what the girl was and what she would do.

In a blink she was in the dark, foggy room of the beyond, the only part of that world she had been so far. Although she knew she was linked to this world, needed this world, she had yet to explore any further than this space. Perhaps there was help here, a way for her to stop the dragon before the dragon could stop her—or worse, assist the boy in reclaiming his crown. When Salima had been just a girl, she had only thought of Ed and being near him. Desperation had driven her, and Ana had at times felt as though the girl was only using her to reach him.

She breathed in the cool, damp air around her and walked forward through the fog, beyond the table and the bed, to find nothing. She huffed and continued forward, but the world didn't change around her. For a moment she wondered if this was all there was, only fog and darkness filled with those who would want to come to the land she had promised them, where all she needed to do was find an anchor to hold them there.

*You are not welcome here. You must remain with the crown.*

Ana's hand moved to the stony points above her head. She screamed out her frustrations, her voice echoing through the fog before it echoed around the throne room. The guard at the door pushed himself back into the wall.

Ana sighed and sat heavily on the throne. There was more to being a queen than this. She held all the power in the world, after all. It was hers and hers alone, and she would not be dictated to, not even by herself.

❋

Dray looked out over the surrounding landscape, wondering how anyone could live so long in such a place without longing for something more. The grasslands appeared to go on forever. There were no hills, no mountains, nothing to lift the eye from the continuous sea of grass before him. Even the cottages and homes were tucked away in the grass, and he wondered if Ed was more comfortable here because of the time he had spent in the marshes.

He wasn't sure at what point he had lost sight of Ana, when he knew that he wouldn't be able to sense her if she appeared before him. It didn't seem so long ago they had left her sitting on a throne of stone beneath the crown she had promised Ed. But whether that loss of connection was something he missed, it certainly appeared to have saved them. For she didn't seem able to find them. Although they had stayed close for several days, in part hoping Ende would return and help them, she hadn't appeared before them. No hint of the girl Dray knew had returned.

He squatted down in the grass, running a blade through his fingers. He had spent enough time working out his frustrations on the grasses around the cottage, slashing them down as Belle had watched him from the doorway. She had said nothing, just watched, and once he had let his frustrations run out, the loss had set in. For Ana was gone, and there was nothing he could do to change that.

"Barlow," Ed said behind him.

"He can't." Dray stood slowly, brushed the grass from his hands and turned. He knew the man wouldn't have come after them. He couldn't.

"He trusted in me."

"And she can see all he does, all he thinks. It isn't even safe for him to consider where we might be, let alone send word. We have covered this."

"Are we sure she knows so much?"

Dray wanted to sigh or shout at the boy, but he couldn't. Someone had to hope there was a better future, and so far, the only one with any hope was Ed. "You have seen what she has done, what she can do."

Ed nodded and looked down at the ground.

"And what she will do to you if she finds you," Dray reminded him.

"I'm surprised that she hasn't. Surely those creatures can go anywhere."

"She doesn't know where to start. And she doesn't seem to just know, as she did before. We have to hope she isn't sending out men."

"Do you think she renamed them?"

Dray laughed, for the first time in so long. The release lifted a weight from his chest. "At least we know she won't have changed the uniform; black seems to be her colour."

Ed gave him a small smile and looked down at his hand, running his thumb over his palm as though trying to remove a mark. Dray watched the movement, one Ed repeated when he was nervous or stressed, which seemed to be most of the time.

"The most important thing for now is to keep you alive," he said. "We can work on a plan later. It has been months, but there is a long way to go."

Ed turned back to the house over his shoulder and then gave Dray a short nod.

"I know I've said this before," Dray said. Ed held up a hand, not raising his eyes to Dray, and Dray stopped, too aware that the king didn't need to hear the words of reassurance again. He didn't need to know that there was time to plan and that they would find a way. Not when Ana's darkness seemed to spread slowly across the kingdom and the people lived in fear. They had moved slowly from the capital and seen so much as they travelled. The death, the intimidation, the punishments she imposed.

The thought of it made him miss Ana all the more. He sucked in a deep breath, trying to curtail the idea. It did no good to think of what might have been; she was gone now, and there was nothing he could do to bring her back. Their focus had to be on finding a way to defeat the witch before the world they knew was gone. Yet he was constantly reminded of her. The day he had met Ana as she carried a tray with tea, looking like a young girl standing in the doorway, staring at him as though he were the most important person in the world. She was gone, he had to keep reminding himself, and the woman who now ruled over the kingdom was not her and never would be again.

Dray looked back at the cottage and couldn't see Belle. "She hasn't said much," he noted.

Ed shook his head, looking again at his hand. Beyond suggesting they go home—her home—Belle had not really spoken at all. He didn't think it had anything to do with what Ed had done in the end to get his crown back from his uncle, even if he had given it away in almost the same instant. Belle hadn't quite been herself, and Dray often wondered if the light Ana had seen in her—and Kemp, for that matter—was something Belle wondered about.

He had yet to see it himself. There was much he hadn't seen that others seemed so attuned to, and yet it was something that was there, some magic he didn't know or understand. He had never fully understood Ana's either. He looked at his own hands then. Ana had been so sure they were slick with blood, and he had fought his share of battles and taken enough lives for that to be the case. And yet, since he had known her, he may have raised his sword to many, but not used it.

Ed focused on his hand, and Dray's fingers found his cheek. There was more to come, more blood to be spilled, and Ana wouldn't be helping them now. She would be standing on the other side of what was to come. They just had to find a way to determine what that was and how they stood a chance. Any chance, for with her shadows and her skills, she would see them coming and destroy any hope.

He looked up beyond the king to the cottage again. "She can't see us coming," he murmured.

"What?" Ed asked, looking back towards the cottage himself. "Belle?"

"Ana," Dray whispered.

"Don't call her that," Belle said, appearing from the grass to his side. He wondered how long she had been hidden nearby and listening. "The creature that sits on the throne, the one who insists on being called Majesty, is not Ana."

Dray felt the overwhelming loss sweep over him again. Belle surprised him by resting a hand on his arm. "She's gone," he murmured.

She nodded once.

He had wanted so desperately to hope there was a chance for Ana, but he knew she was gone forever. She hadn't been consumed by whatever magic she had; she was that magic. This was who Ana was, and it might be that the girl he knew, the girl he would have given his life to protect, had never existed in the first place.

"The connection is gone," Belle continued quietly. "I think you are right. She won't see you coming."

"But we can't just appear in the capital. She will have us killed, or worse, turned into one of her shadow soldiers. I think the last of Ana, whatever might have been, allowed us to walk out of that room, but she will do everything she can to ensure we don't walk back in."

"Dray thinks just keeping me safe is enough," Ed said, allowing Belle to take his hand and lead them back towards the cottage.

"He has kept you safe for months. Maybe now is the time to consider what we do next."

Ed shook his head slowly. Dray wondered if he really didn't want to try to get his throne back, if he didn't want to take on Ana or if the confidence he had seen in the young man had simply vanished.

As they entered the small cottage, Master Forest stood over a pot on the fire, stirring slowly, his gaze focused on some distant spot. Dray knew where his thoughts were, on his daughter Salima lost somewhere with Ende.

Dray wasn't as concerned for the girl as her father was. There was something very special about the little dragon, and he knew she would return to them when she could, when she knew they needed her. Maybe they should simply wait for that time. But he had suggested something similar when they had first left the capital, and it hadn't been received well, so he kept the idea to himself.

"Stew," Forest said, lifting the spoon out to taste the contents.

"We always have stew," Ed murmured. Phillip lifted himself slowly from the chair and carried a bowl toward the fire. "I like stew," he added when the older man glanced his way. They had limited options, and Dray felt like they hadn't eaten a decent meal since before he'd left the barracks for Sheer Rock with the mage so long ago. Although they had eaten meat in the mountains. And at the inn.

As Belle sat the watery stew down before him at the table, Dray thought he hadn't taken enough notice of what was important as they had travelled, that he hadn't paid enough attention to those around him. Belle's hand rested on his shoulder, and he looked into her blue eyes as she gave him a small smile. He tried to return it but found his lips wouldn't quite move as he wanted them to. He put his hand over hers and patted it instead. She was kind. As Ed cleared his throat and glared across the table, Dray found his smile, removed his hand and started to eat.

# 2

Salima stretched lazily across the hot rocks and rolled onto her back. She sighed with contentment, blowing out a long fiery breath. It was only at Ende's growl that she opened her eyes to the bright sun and looked around at him. Despite his assurances that he was a dragon and not a man, he had chosen to look like a human most of the time. Salima, on the other hand, enjoyed exploring her dragon form. It soaked up the heat of the sun and the rocks much more efficiently.

She reluctantly returned to her human form. She didn't need to change to communicate with Ende, and yet he preferred it. In the months they had been hiding in the hot, dry rocky mountains of the desert region of Ilia, she had learnt far more about herself than she had in all the years she had lived as a girl.

She was also stronger than she had realised, and more skilled in some things than Ende. Her ability to read people was one of those areas. He had such a skill himself, but Salima only need look and she could see their futures blurring ahead of them. Some aspects were clear and crisp, others not so much.

"Were you thinking of him again?" Ende asked.

She had been trying not to. She had been so focused on Ed for so very long, and it was only after she had seen him in the shop that last time that Dray had stolen her attention. Dray knew what she was; he had seen it in the room and understood it in the street. There were moments when she wasn't sure if it was his connection to Ana that allowed this or if he had a skill of his own, but it meant something. He meant something. Dray would be a key to end this story, although she wasn't clear on what that was yet.

"Do you worry about him?" Ende prompted.

"No. He can look after himself well enough."

"Truly?" Ende asked, and she turned to take him in.

"You are talking of Ed," she said matter-of-factly. "I am talking of the captain."

He raised his eyebrows, and she smiled.

"I have seen him," she said, turning her gaze from Ende out across the sand that stretched away from them. In the distance, she could feel the moist earth of the grasslands. She knew he was not far from her, but he didn't need her now. None of them needed her now. They would, but they needed to find themselves first.

She wondered at her new thinking. It hadn't been so long ago that she'd needed to protect Ed with everything she had, that nothing had been as important as him. And yet she sensed the world so differently now that she had found the fire within. "Did I share in your wisdom when I became a dragon?" she asked, turning back to the man sitting straight backed on the rock beside her, his hands on his knees.

"You were always a dragon," he said with a smile that warmed her heart. "Why do you ask about wisdom? There would be many who would say I am somewhat lacking."

She laughed easily and reached out to rest her hand on his. "I feel somewhat different, older and yet not at the same time. I might have claimed not to be a girl. But it is as though I now know I am no longer a girl."

"You have seen much," he said softly, looking at her hand. "You are gifted, and with that a level of understanding comes."

She breathed in the warmth around her and blew out a soft breath. "So much has changed," she whispered. "So much is not as I thought it was or would be. There is so much to come."

"Do you want to be with Ed?"

"He will need me, but he needs to find himself first."

"Will you tell me of Dray?"

"I'm not sure that I see it all." She pulled away from him and walked to the edge of the cliff. "I'm not always sure of what I have seen." She ran a finger over her cheek, feeling the warm, wet blood drip from the stinging gash as though it were her own. In the same instant, she felt the pain and loss of Ana. Salima closed her eyes and thought of the woman she had wanted to be so close to. She knew with certainty that Ana would still cause so much pain.

"I saw what she would become, that she would betray them, and yet I couldn't stop it," Ende said.

"You weren't meant to," Salima said, looking out over the world. "It was destined to go this way."

"Destiny can be shifted."

She turned back and looked at him seriously. "Don't be naive, Endeavour. We cannot change what is destined to be."

He blinked at her slowly. "You believe the world should be in chaos, with a witch working to destroy it."

She nodded once. "For now, the future is blurry, but what is clear is right." She touched her hand to her cheek once more and then leapt from the cliff, changing form almost instantly and then soaring across the hot sand, enjoying the heat of the sun on her back.

The mage sucked in a breath as the creature appeared before his desk. Although he had gotten much better at appearing calmer than he felt, he knew the creature sensed far more than he wished. He tried to study the dusty pages of the book open before him. Their tightly written, faded script was taking most of his concentration to read.

"Majesty would like you to seek out the boy."

"I've tried," he said without looking up. "I couldn't do it before he returned as King. Why would it be any different now?"

The creature growled, the low noise making the mage's heart race and the walls shudder.

He put down the quill he had been twirling between his fingers, for he was sure holding it helped him think more clearly, and stared up at the round, dark eyes focused only on him. He had no idea if this creature had been his maid or was formed from someone else. She had made so many more of them, and although she didn't appear to call them anything other than "child," they appeared to know which was which.

"I have searched. I have tried," he said. He wouldn't dare go against her. She hadn't threatened him as yet, but she didn't need to. He saw all too clearly what she did and how she did it. If he tried to defy her, she would know instantly. He wanted to regret bringing her here, wanted to agree that the regent had been right. Not that he could demand such from him now. He too was lost to the darkness she had brought to the kingdom, a darkness he had allowed her to find.

He smiled up at the creature before him, and it narrowed its eyes. "I will try again," he said, looking back to the page. In many ways, he was proud. She had become just as he'd thought she would, which meant he couldn't doubt himself and his own skill. And she had found such a way under his tutelage. If he could call it that. He should have paid her more attention when he'd had the chance and he might be sitting beside her.

The growl caught him unawares. He cleared his throat before looking up to find the creature gone. He sighed with relief, but he couldn't allow himself the time to relax. She might send another, and he had much to do.

Mariela had written down her experience of the beyond before she had disappeared. Before the creature had taken her over. Although she had fought, it hadn't been enough. The only way had been to separate them and record the experience in the hope that he could try again later. But he had lost the woman, and the creature had fought so violently until he'd managed to trap it in the book. Looking over her notes, he had found very little to help him in his current proximity to shadows, but it had sparked a memory of something similar he had read written many hundreds of years before, and he had finally found where he had read it.

Yet it was difficult to decipher. The text was faded and written hurriedly, as though the mage with the quill had too little time to write it all down. The words ran into each other, the letters sometimes not properly formed. There was no history of the kingdom or even a part of it being lost to darkness as it appeared to be now. No dark creature sat on the throne; no one sent creatures through the world to do her bidding.

And he had yet to find an answer for how to slow her down or stop her. He was curious to see how far she would go, what she would do to maintain her hold—although it appeared that was taking very little effort on her part. There was a strength to her, something new that he hadn't quite sensed before. She had made the creatures, called them, given them life, forced others to do as they were bid. But that wasn't just the darkness. She could see inside a man, know his thoughts, his motivations. She knew when they lied to her, when they tried to hide from her. It had taken some time for the kingdom to fall in line, but once they had realised just how strong she was, they had bowed down before her.

The mage needed answers, but he didn't think the king was one of those. Finding him would placate the witch, but the mage couldn't put him back on the throne even if he wanted to. The boy would want him dead, just as he did his uncle, given what he had done to help destroy his father and bring the regent to power. Not to mention his having helped the regent steal Ana away in the first place.

The text before him blurred further, as though someone had wet the page, and he turned the page to find it was blank. He turned more, crinkled as the others were, as though shaped by ink that wasn't there. He sighed and ran his fingers over the old paper. It was almost crisp beneath his skin. He closed his eyes and tried to sense something in the old pages, but there was nothing. He looked up and around the space he knew as home and wondered for the first time who would follow him here.

He'd had many students over the years, some for longer times, some for very short. Some he had brought here just to see what they could do and what use they would be to him. He had followed in a long line of strong mages who had left their history and knowledge amongst the piles of books and bottles on the shelves. There was something in Ana. Something had drawn him in, and he hadn't even considered her his successor. He pushed up from the book and breathed in the scent of so many who had come before. For the first time he felt old, as though he might not live forever. For he had wanted such a thing at some point. And this would all be lost.

Looking into the dark corners of the room, he thought of the shadows and how they had shied away from the light. Sarah had been a light, and for a moment he wondered where she might have gone. Her sister, whatever she had become, had taken what was hers and the light had gone out, but the shadows had wanted her all the same. They were supposed to be his, yet the creature had won out. Ana had made her promises, and they would do as they were told.

He walked away from the book, searching the shelves. He had light captured in nearly every form within this very room, but it would take a particular light. He stood before a shelf, running his finger over the labels before him and wondering how he had aged so quickly, his finger thin and bony, his pointed nails tapping over the glass vials.

The king's little companion came to mind. With her blond shiny hair, her glowing skin. She had a light. She was something Ana had seen, yet she had not touched her. Did Ana not think her a threat? Did Ana think the girl wouldn't dare harm the friend she had been to them?

Would they try to save the girl who was no more? He tapped against the bottle beneath his finger and the contents screamed, but he wouldn't touch them for they weren't what he needed. He needed the king's friend, for the light she had. He sighed and turned back to his desk and the book open there, the candlelight illuminating the still-blank pages. He would have to find the king. He would need to bring them back to the capital, all of them. And he would need to do it without his new queen discovering what he planned. She wanted the king, and the mage would find him.

He thought something blinked in the darkness beyond the candlelight of his desk. But he wasn't sure. Could they all read him as she did? Could they all see deep into the minds of men?

"Yes," hissed in his ear. He turned suddenly, his heart beating too fast, and then staggered back, bumping into the shelf. The bottles clinked and squealed as they were knocked together. In the following silence, the mage searched the room for any sign of the creature that had been watching him. But he couldn't see it. Couldn't see any sign of something present. But it was here. They were always watching.

# 3

The queen rested back in her throne as the shadows whispered over her skin. She wasn't worried about the mage or what he might do. The old man didn't have nearly the same power she did. There was a time he might have been a threat, but he was no longer. He would find what she had asked of him as he searched out a way to stop her.

The king, the boy, was hiding. They were hiding, and she wanted to ensure he wouldn't try anything. She had listened from the shadows and not even heard a whisper to indicate that he might act against her or was trying to win his people back. He wouldn't dare, not now. Not when they knew what she was and what she could do. She just needed to be sure.

A shadow formed into one of her children before her. It bent slowly, still awkward in this world, as though it didn't belong, and yet Ana felt more comfortable every day. The child before her had once been a soldier, Kemp.

"They travel to the forest in search of the boy," he hissed, the two creatures that had joined now one, as many of them had become now she was Queen of this world.

"The Lord of Near Forest was not happy when he left, and he may have heard what happened to his sister and her husband. Would he allow them sanctuary?" she asked.

"The Near Folk might," the child hissed.

Ana had forgotten the Near Folk. She had felt their magic in the trees, and yet had not really learnt who they were. She had grown up believing them a myth, but so much that she would not have believed before, made sense now.

"Might?" Ana leaned forward. The child before her lifted dark eyes and nodded once. "Why are you not certain?"

"The trees are preventing our entry."

"Shadows can go anywhere—they are everywhere," she said, trying hard to keep her voice level. She had managed to infiltrate every part of the kingdom, so how were they not in the trees? "Were they seen entering?"

The child shook his head once.

"Then Barlow is guessing."

"Or he is leading us away from them," the child hissed. "The dragons…"

She held up a hand and silenced the child before her, then nodded once. She didn't know where the dragons were either, but she had an idea they were somewhere far from her reach. They would return when the little one thought she could help her brother. Ana pushed up from the throne and stepped down from the raised platform. The child before her disappeared as she continued along the length of the room and out into the courtyard.

People moved around the space, quiet and eyes down. She usually blinked from place to place rather than walk, but she stepped out into the sunshine and squinted at the blue sky. She could sense those around her wondering what she was doing, fearing what she might do and waiting for her to blink from existence again.

*If the dragon thought her brother was in danger, she would have come with him to the throne room that day.*

"But she left instead." Salima had made that choice, just as she would be the one to return. Ana wondered then what she had seen, what skill the little one had of her father's that would lead her back to help the brother she had left behind.

She felt the fear and relief from those in the courtyard as she blinked out of the sunshine and to the balcony in her room. The royal suite. The shadows cooled her as she stood and looked over the world before her. No matter what the dragon thought she was, Ana was too strong to be worried by it.

A creature, child, appeared beside her.

"Ruth," Ana said without turning from the view. "Hide yourself among the people, go to the trees, find the Near Folk and determine what they do. Find the boy and return him to me."

Ruth bowed. Although Ana hadn't used the name of the child she had been for some time, this one still had skills her other children did not have. Including the first who had come, the one who had taken Ruth's sister.

"Go," Ana growled when the child remained beside her, taking advantage of her distraction.

"Majesty," she hissed. She paused a moment longer, as though wanting to ask or share something, but was gone before Ana could determine what that might be.

The children also felt the world around them, the thoughts of the men they were surrounded by, and although they shared what they learnt, there was something of those men Ana could sense in her children. Something human had crept into the creatures they had become. They had been something very separate and yet joined before she was Queen. Now they were solid shadow, what had once been man and beast now one creature, one child of the shadows. If they didn't follow her direction, then they would see the same fate of the men who had tried to stand against her.

Despite any doubts, she understood the child would do her bidding, no matter what was asked or what it might cost her. The view across the city was both beautiful and frustrating. As comfortable as Ana was in this world, she couldn't linger in the sun as she would have before. The bright midday light she had squinted into in the courtyard reflected from every building before her and appeared to intensify. Her children were enough to keep the populace in place, but she wondered if there was a way around it. A way they had found to get around her.

She leaned forward into the little sun that reached the edge of the balcony and breathed in the despair rising from the buildings below. They knew the boy would never return, and that he could not win his crown back if he did.

But others might have hope hidden. She wondered if she would find them out. Barlow had headed for the trees. Was it because he truly thought the boy was there, or did he think they would protect him? He hadn't been exposed to the Near Folk when he had gone to collect the tribute.

Ana blinked away from the balcony and, in a breath, she was standing in the small attic room that had not so long ago housed

Dray and Ed and Belle, protected by the King's Men. She had placed Ed here herself, sent him with one of the children. The space was empty and just as covered in dust as when she had first seen it. She had no idea where the beds had gone, and she didn't care. It was as it had been when Dray had first arrived here.

*You cannot leave your throne.*

"Who would take it?" she growled. "Why such fear for what is mine? The whole kingdom is mine, and so it is assured."

Silence followed. Despite her understanding of the world around her and what power she had from beyond, Ana knew deep in her soul that there was more to her magic than she might ever understand, more than it would share with her.

She wanted to hold in the rage she felt building beneath her skin, but it burned hotter than she imagined. The shadows moved and twisted around her. She wanted something to take that frustration out on, something or someone to punish. She thought of Dray and his disappointment when she had taken the crown. She closed her eyes, but when she opened them, she was in the same dusty room and he wasn't there.

*He is mine,* the voice inside her hissed. The anger curled up from her stomach and tightened around her throat.

"He was never yours, and he will never be." Ana clawed at her throat. "If I die, you die," she wheezed.

The constriction released instantly. She sucked in a deep breath and extended her hands out to the side, pushing down the walls.

The roof crashed down around her, people screamed out in the street as stonework rained down on unsuspecting passersby. The small part of roof was held above her by the shadows. Ana grinned, and then a bubble of laughter started in her throat and she could not contain it. The more she laughed, the more the anger inside her grew. Then Ana stepped out into the light, and the roof fell with a crash to the floor she had been standing on.

The whole building creaked loudly, as though it might all slip to the ground in a pile of rubble.

"I am the queen," she hissed, the sound filling the world around her, echoing from the surrounding buildings. The following silence was deafening. "I am Majesty, not you. You are nothing."

*You would be nothing without me. You are Queen because I am Majesty. I have done so much to put you on the throne and the crown on your head. You would do well to remember that. He was always mine. And he will ensure the people bow to me.*

"Then bring him forth," Ana said sweetly. "If you can bring him here, now, to this very place, you can keep him. If not, we will speak of it no more."

Ana closed her eyes, feeling the world sway around her as the magic inside her grew and burned and reached out through the shadows. She looked out when nothing changed and, with a nod to the shadows around her, she was lifted from the damaged floor and landed softly in the street just as the building dissolved into rubble behind her.

She felt the frustration as the magic searched for something Ana knew she would never find. "Enough."

The magic stopped, the heat dissipating, and Ana sighed with relief. "You are mine," she said, walking back through the cool streets where the tall edges of the buildings or their overhanging roofs protected her from the direct rays of the sun.

People scurried out of the way, and she smiled and bowed her head to those who stopped and curtsied or bowed as she passed.

*Together we are Majesty,* a begrudging voice whispered in the darkness at the back of her mind.

# 4

Dray stood slowly. For a moment, just a moment, he thought he felt Ana, sensed her as he had when she hid in the shadows. But it passed just as quickly; it must have been the idea of her. Yet there was a pull. He stepped away from the small table and to the doorway of the cottage, the meal forgotten on the table behind him. By the time he put his hand to the latch, the feeling was gone. He turned back to the small group staring at him from the table.

"Has something happened?" Ed asked.

He shook his head.

"Have you an idea of what we do next?" Phillip tried.

Dray opened his mouth and then closed it.

"Ana," Belle whispered, still looking at her plate.

"I thought so, but then no—it wasn't her."

"Something called to you," Belle continued, her eyes not meeting his. A strange chill covered his skin.

He reached the table in two large strides and leant over it, his hands firmly planted on either side of his plate as he stared at the woman focused on her plate on the opposite side. Ed had leaned away from him as he reached the table, and he growled something Dray didn't quite hear. No one else spoke. No one moved except Belle, who was pushing the watery stew around her plate.

"What are you?" he asked.

"I don't know."

The sorrow that filled her voice and the lone tear that dripped into the already watery stew made him sit back on the bench beside his king. But he couldn't take his eyes from the young woman who had confused him so often before. She had been annoying and clinging, frightened and strong, bright and articulate. She had swayed the heart of a king. But when Dray glanced at the boy beside him, clearly unsure what to do to comfort the woman, he was sure it was the boy from the forest who had fallen for her and not just her beauty. Her father moved, sliding along the bench and wrapping his arm around her, pulling her close, and she rested her head on his shoulder.

Dray expected more tears, for her to sob, but she didn't. If it weren't for the wet line that tracked down her cheek, he would have thought her calm and resting. "I'm sorry," he found himself saying, unsure what he was apologising for. He had only wondered what she was. For she had a magic, one that he didn't understand, but Ana had seen. She understood that some distant connection to Ana had just pulled at him, even though he wasn't sure he felt it himself.

In that moment, he wanted to hope that Ana was still inside the creature who was Queen. But it hadn't quite been her. Even when he had sensed her in the shadows, he had understood that it was her with her magic, but this wasn't even that. "It wasn't Ana," he whispered.

"No," Belle said, looking up from her father's shoulder. "I think she has gone, but it was something connected to her in some way."

"It felt wrong," he said, unsure how to describe what he had felt before, and so even more unsure how to describe the difference from that.

Belle nodded.

"You felt it," he said, standing again. This time she looked at him, eyes following as he stood. "Do you know what she is?"

"I don't understand myself enough."

Ed opened his mouth and then closed it. She moved her focus to him, smiling a little and reaching out her hand across the table. He took it quickly, as though she might pull away if he didn't take it right then. She shook her head just a little as Dray studied her, and then she sighed.

"The light," Dray said.

She looked up again, and he moved away from the table.

"We need more understanding. We need more friends."

"What do you have in mind?" Ed asked. When Dray turned

back towards the table, the king was grinning at him.

"You seem confident," Dray said.

"He knows you will have a plan," Belle added.

"I haven't been very good at that so far."

"I think we could claim you somewhat distracted," Phillip murmured.

Ed's smile faltered, and Belle grumbled something.

"The Near Folk," Dray said quickly. "They are a part of this kingdom and yet not. They have an understanding of magic; they were even willing to share what they had with Ana. Maybe they can help us understand what has happened, help us find a way to…"

"We can't get her back," Belle interrupted.

"No," Dray admitted, any hope he had disappearing. "Maybe they can help us find a way to defeat her."

Ed gulped down whatever words had been forming on his lips and raised his eyebrows as he turned to Belle.

"I know Ana has gone," Dray said, unable to move his feet at all. "I know there is no hope for her. She is gone, she is dead." The word caught in his throat.

Belle nodded slowly, and Ed looked down at the table. Phillip nudged his daughter aside, stood and came around to take Dray by the arms.

"I am sorry," he said, and Dray could see the truth of it in his eyes. He nodded slowly.

"We need help. We need an army, and one that can find a way into the capital without alerting her soldiers we are there."

"I agree," Ed said, sitting taller. "It is time to fight back. The Near Folk might be the best option, other than…" He chewed on his lip, but Dray knew what he was thinking.

"Salima will find us when the time is right."

"How do we reach the forest without them finding us?" Ed asked. "We stand no chance in the open."

Dray sighed. The end goal was right, but making it there alive could be a challenge. "I did say I wasn't so good at plans."

"Her connection to you appears to be broken," Belle said softly, looking between the two of them. "But her creatures could still find you by your thoughts alone. How can we think something very different from what we want?"

Ed huffed and Phillip stood back, his arms dropping by his sides. Dray wondered whether the Near Folk could come to them, but he doubted they would leave the trees.

Barlow pushed the horse harder, and the men behind him only just managed to keep up. As they crossed the threshold of the Near Forest, the shadows around him screamed in frustration. He knew they travelled with him—they were always close—but he hadn't seen them since they'd left the capital.

Barlow breathed a sigh of relief, as though a weight had been lifted from his chest and his mind. It was almost as though he were free. The shadows growled and hissed, and he urged his horse forward slowly.

"They can't follow," he whispered. The men around him grinned.

He had taken three men with him, men he had once trusted, although Kemp came to mind. Barlow had trusted him to not only work with Sterling, but watch over the king. Instead he had tried to kill them, or at least Sterling. The retelling hadn't been clear. The loss of the man was his only understanding of the situation at the time, and he had no idea which one of the children might be him, if he even still existed. She could destroy them as easily as she did any man who went against her.

It had been hard to maintain the façade of searching for the king to the north. If he had any sense, he would have gone south towards the desert, for the creatures couldn't survive the blinding sun as well as they did the cool shadows. The new queen had ensured her world was comfortable for her, creating shade. And then she would appear in full sunlight and scare him even more. She did it for the reaction, he had realised, feeding off the fear and uncertainty of the people around her. And it was hard not to fear her.

Whenever she mentioned the king—the boy, she called him— Barlow would remember him as he had seen him that day in the trees. The confident young man who looked so much like his father. Barlow wondered why he hadn't done anything to assist the young king sooner. But the trees. He only ever let the trees come to mind, and so when she had asked for him to find the boy, he had headed straight for the trees.

He was relieved now that they couldn't follow him, and he wondered if there was a magic in the forest that would protect them. The king had talked of it himself at one stage. Although, what the Lord of Near Forest would think of the King's Men—now shadow soldiers although thankfully not shadows—appearing in his province after the death of his sister, Barlow couldn't guess.

He headed for the lord's seat. He wasn't even sure if the man knew what had happened in relation to his sister, or if he should. The others followed behind, maintaining the silence they had all become used to of late.

# 5

Ana stood in the doorway of the mage's workroom and breathed in the odd scent that filled it. When she had lived here not so very long ago, she had grown used to it. But now, as when she had first met the mage, she was very aware of it. And more frustratingly, she still could not place the scent. It was familiar and yet unnamed.

She stepped forward into the dark space, wondering where the old man was hiding and what he might be planning. The shadows thought him a threat, that he wanted to save the king, but he would do her work and hunt him out. She had asked it of him, after all; he just didn't want to. Now he would, thinking it was for his own reasons.

A book was open on his desk, and she leaned over the empty pages. She turned them back a few and looked over the tight script. It was faded and hard to read. She placed her hand on the page and closed her eyes.

The words rearranged themselves within her mind, and then the image of a woman appeared. She was very beautiful. As Ana watched, the shadows closed in around her and she was consumed. Ana wondered for a moment if this was someone's eyewitness account of such an event. Like the book beneath her fingers, it felt like long ago.

The creature stepped from the shadows, and Ana could feel them both, as she did her own shadows. But there was something else, something different, as though the woman within was stronger, not as willing to accept the change. The struggle was painful. Ana winced, the shadows shifted and the woman dropped to her knees. She was alone. Somehow, she had defeated the shadows.

Ana stepped back. Confusion filled her.

*We can be separated.*

"No. She might have been strong, but that is not something the mage can do."

*He is trying to find a way.*

Ana could feel the panic of the magic within her. The uncertainty of what her life would be, separated from it. It would be nothing. She would be nothing, and that was not a way to live. He had brought the shadows here. He had created the first creature. Somewhere within this place was the secret to his success. The reason he appeared stronger than she was. For she knew it wasn't true. The old man could not have more power than she did.

"Where is the way?" she murmured, looking through the books that littered the desk.

*Search for the shadows, search for what lies beyond.*

Ana stood tall and closed her eyes again. The bottles on the shelves appeared to hold their collective breath. They had not made a sound since she had entered the space. She took a small step closer to a set of shelves, hoping to force a noise, but the tense silence continued. She reached out further with her senses. The bottles, the items, the books all contained something of the beyond, something of the shadows. But there was more.

She took a deep breath and noticed an absence of shadows in a book in a pile on the floor not far from the desk. She had seen it before when she had snapped her finger and it had appeared atop the other book. Its pages opened, and nothing was contained within. She had touched those pages, taken an ink image of a queen from amongst them. Had he managed to remove the shadows from the book?

Her magic cried out in pain. She clutched at her chest, leaning forward and placing her hand on the brittle pages.

*Trapped,* whispered through her mind.

"Was a shadow trapped here?"

She felt the confirmation.

"Trapped against its will," Ana whispered, and the room erupted in a cacophony of noise. Bottles rattled, shelves squeaked, contents called out. "You are all trapped," she said, looking around the room. How had he taken so much from the beyond? "What would you do if I freed you?"

*No.* The voice inside her was calm, in control once more. *That is not what they need of their queen.*

Ana placed her hand back on the pages of the book before her. "He took the shadow from someone, from a creature, from someone like us."

Silence filled the world around her. The shelves were silent, her magic as well.

"Mother," she whispered. "He took Mother's magic. But then where did she go?"

Ana looked around the room as though she might still be present, although she wasn't sure what she would do if faced with her. Ana's heart stopped. A cold chill took over her whole frame. The mage had given that magic, that shadow, to someone else. The maid had been formed from what had been her mother.

The white-hot anger that had destroyed the building returned, pushing out into the room, causing the bottles and the world to squeal and scream again. Ana called the child forth, and it appeared before her. There was something else within the grin that formed on the wide face as the black tongue flicked over it, and Ana scowled.

Ana held up a finger and it bent slowly, bowing low before her, but it should have dropped to its knees. Ana took a deep breath and placed her hands on the cool, smooth head of the child. As with her other children, it was one, the maid absorbed. Her coming here had changed things. They were no longer two creatures, two souls bound—they were one.

"He cannot separate us," she breathed, relief flooding through her at the realisation.

"Majesty, you have gifted so much," the child hissed. Ana tried again to sense the difference. It wasn't that they had joined; there was something more. A strength this creature contained.

"Do you still want to destroy me?" Ana asked.

"Never, Majesty. I would help you. I would offer my new strength to ensure your continued reign."

"The child of light?"

"I put out the light."

Ana waited, but the creature said no more. There was no sign of the child within her, but it was now complete. There was more to Ana than her magic, more to her than the creature within. Could this creature have developed something from what she had taken?

"Her sister took the light," the creature hissed, as though understanding what Ana thought. Although she knew they could do that with others, they should not have been able to read her. She was their queen, after all. Not some man in the market who might become a soldier to help her.

Ruth didn't appear any different, although she could still appear as whatever or whoever she wanted. Ana wondered if Ruth could appear as her sister. But then, there was no need. Her appearing as King Barric had been clever enough, taking the thoughts of the regent and twisting them, twisting the situation to what she needed it to be for Ed to hand her the crown. He had given her just what she'd wanted, and the people had to accept her. If the king had deemed it necessary to give the crown to her, what could they do? She was too strong for them to take on themselves. And if he wouldn't fight, neither would they.

"What happened to my mother?" Ana was not sure she wanted the answer, but she needed to know if the mage had the power she suspected he did.

The creature before her blinked, but remained silent.

"You were connected to her. You were trapped in the book," she said, placing her hand down slowly over the paper.

"I am more than the shadows called," the child hissed, bowing low again. "What was before has gone."

Ana reached forward again and put her hands to the creature's face. It dropped to its knees with a wail of pain. She searched for the shadows it had been before, but she had done more than create a solid creature anchored here—she had lost what it had been before it had become hers.

Ana sighed out her frustrations.

*You don't need her. You are stronger than she ever was.*

"I know that. I need to ensure he cannot separate us." The child on the floor looked up at her and blinked slowly with large dark eyes. "I could separate you if I chose, but it is not what I want. Where has the old man gone?"

"To do your bidding, Majesty."

"Has he too headed for the forest? Would the boy be so

predictable?"

"Why seek him, Majesty?"

Ana arched an eyebrow, but the child didn't look away. It was right, as her magic had been. She didn't need any of them, and she certainly didn't need to fear any of them. She had allowed them to live, but they wouldn't be stupid enough to think they could best her. They had seen what she was, what power she commanded, the soldiers she would use on them and the people.

Yet there was an uncertainty. With him still out there in the world, there was the risk of his return. The risk of his attempt to take back what was his. And she couldn't have that. Not when she had worked so hard to make the kingdom hers.

# 6

Belle hid out in the long grass, sitting down amongst the green stalks and breathing in their sweet scent. She had missed the crops when she had been dragged away to the forest. She hadn't thought she ever would, but she had far more than she realised. And even after all their travels and her certainty that she wanted to be wherever Ed was, this was home. This sweet scent was home.

She knew they would be looking for her. Dray had seen something in her the previous day, understood that there was a magic within her somewhere and she could only hope it wasn't like Ana's. And yet, somewhere deep within her, Belle knew it was very different.

There was something in the girl who had shone brightly in the throne room. She had sensed the pain the light had caused the shadow creatures and Ana. But although she sensed it and in some small way understood it, she hadn't been able to replicate it.

Ana had told her not to shine, but Ana might have sensed the power within her more than seen it. If she had truly thought Belle a threat, she would have fed her to one of the creatures as she had the girl. Belle shivered at the idea and tried to calm the fast beating of her heart.

She turned back towards the cottage. She heard Ed calling to her from somewhere in the distance, but she remained where she was, sitting silent in the grass. He wouldn't be able to track her through the crop. She knew how to tread lightly through the tall stalks. She always knew where he was when he headed out into the fields, leaving wide tracks of pushed-down stalks in his wake.

Belle looked up to fragments of clear blue sky through the soft green edges of the tall stalks. She had waited for a sign of the dragons, for Salima to hunt them out as she had before. But in all the months they had been hiding at the farm, there had been no sign of her or Ende. She wondered then if there was nothing for them to come for. If they knew there was no hope for Ed to regain his crown, or for them to have a life away from the farm. Not that she really wanted that now. She would be content to just stay here, hidden in the grass.

She wanted to be with Ed, but where his place in the world was now, she couldn't be sure. Even Dray had appeared to take to the life of a farmer and helped her father whenever he could. But he was a mixture of emotions that pulled at Belle. She hadn't thought she would be able to read the big, silent soldier, but now she felt the confusion, the conflict in his loss of Ana and the distant hope that she could be saved. She'd had that feeling herself. And then there was Master Forest, a man very worried for his daughter, understanding that she couldn't be close while still fearful of what she had become.

That was something Dray was clear on, that Salima needed to be away for now and would know when to return. Did she really need to return? Did she really know when she would be needed? Would she know what she was needed for?

Belle took a calming breath, dragging in the sweet scent of the grass, and stood. Sensing something else, she turned slowly. Dray stood silently in the grass, watching her.

"Have you worked out what you are?"

She shook her head. "Can you tell me what you know of Salima?"

He nodded once, and she motioned to the small space she had created in the grass stalks. He smiled as he sat down. She sat beside him, shoulder to shoulder, realising just how broad a man he was.

"This is nice," he said, looking around and taking a deep breath. "I can see why you came out here. Is this where you hide?"

She nodded once without turning to look at him.

"Salima," he started quietly, "has her father's gifts. And may even be stronger than he is, despite not being fully dragon."

Belle waited.

Dray locked his fingers and sat his hands on his knees. "At the shop, she discovered that she could see things. See the future or what it might be."

Belle looked at him more closely, taking in his serious features and wondering if he was not quite telling the truth. But she doubted this man would lie to her.

"She didn't tell me what she saw, but she understood she had to leave. Whether that was to protect herself or Ed, I couldn't tell you. But she will return. She knows there will come a time she is needed to help Ed, and she will come back."

"Is that all she said?"

He nodded.

"But you know more," Belle prompted.

"I don't know what she saw, but I could tell she saw something of everyone in that room, including you." He turned then to take her in, his face soft and friendly, his eyes crinkling with his smile. "I believe she is looking after us all by leaving us."

Belle nodded, not because she thought he might be right, but because she believed he understood the words to be true. "Ende saw something dangerous in Ana. He knew she would not be what we hoped."

Dray nodded again, looking at his hands, and she felt his sadness. She reached out and placed a hand on his arm.

"I'm sorry," she murmured.

"It was what it was always going to be, perhaps, and nothing I could do to try and save her would ever work. Sometimes I wonder what the world would be if I had let her fall."

Belle leaned into the man, resting her head against his shoulder. "You would never have done that, whether she had called to you or not. You were always meant to save her."

He huffed and took a ragged breath. Belle half thought he was crying. "I don't think I ever could have saved her, no matter what I was willing to give to make it happen. But I care for her still, no matter what she is or what she might be. We are going to have to stand against her at some point, for Ed, and I don't know how to do that." His voice was surprisingly level.

"Together," Belle whispered. "We'll work it out together."

"What are you doing?" Ed snapped, appearing in the small clearing. Belle sighed, not at the interruption, but at the track of broken stalks behind him.

"Formulating a plan," she said, brushing at her skirts as she stood. Then she held up her hand to Ed, halting any further movement through the grass. "I think you have pushed down enough of the crop."

He looked around behind him and then back to Dray, who was slowly climbing to his feet. Belle tried not to sigh as he turned back to her with raised eyebrows. She shook her head once and pushed past him and along the path he had created through the grass back towards the cottage.

"A plan?" he asked, moving quickly behind her. He took her arm to halt her and pulled her back towards him. "One without me, with the two of you hiding in the grass?"

She looked back over his shoulder, expecting the big man to say something, but he had disappeared. She smiled, surprised that he could move so silently and easily through the grass.

She looked back at Ed's scowl. "This is silly," she said, pulling from his hold to move back to the cottage.

"Is he a better man than me?" he asked, and the fear in his voice made her stop.

She didn't know how she could reassure him. She had developed a friendship with Dray and was surprised it made Ed uncomfortable. "He is your friend," she said.

"He is a soldier," he murmured.

She blinked up at him, taking a step closer, trying to read the emotions and failing. She looked down, uncertainty washing over her.

"I am King," he said, his voice firm and confident.

"Yes, Your Majesty," she said, trying to place where she was, what she was doing, what he wanted to use her for. She gave a shallow curtsy and turned back to the cottage.

He ran after her, catching her quickly, throwing his arms around her shoulders and holding her close to his chest. She could feel the fast beat of his heart against her back. Selfishness and want flowed around her from him.

"What do you want?" she asked. The words sounded harsher than she intended, but she couldn't hide her disappointment that he didn't think of her as she did him.

"Belle?" He loosened his hold, and she stepped away from him before turning back and bowing her head.

"I am sorry, Your Majesty," she said.

"Don't do that." He stepped forward, but she took a step back.

"I am just a farmer's daughter," she said, looking down. "I was mistaken to think I could be more."

"You are far more than I ever thought possible," he said, the lost boy from the mountains seeming to reappear before her. The odd feeling dissipated, and she dropped to her knees.

"Belle…" He crouched beside her, wrapped his arms around her and pulled her to his chest. "I'm sorry."

She sucked in a deep breath, taking in the scent of the man wrapped around her, and leaned into him. "If he is not your friend, what am I?"

"He is my friend, and a better friend than I deserve. He lost Ana—we all lost Ana," he added quickly, "but he seemed to lose more."

Belle nodded against him. She understood that very clearly.

"I don't want…"

Belle leaned back and looked over the man, the king, before her. She closed her eyes and blew out a soft breath, trying to remove all the uncertainty surrounding her. It didn't really work, but she understood he was just as uncertain of what was to come.

"He thinks Salima understands what is to come," she said softly.

"Do you care for him?"

She smiled as she ran a hand over Ed's face. "He is my friend."

Ed nodded slowly, and she leant forward and put her lips to his. When he didn't respond, she pulled back and allowed her hand to drop from his face.

"You didn't explain what I was," Belle said, looking down at the crushed grass around her knees, the green stains on her skirts, her hands all too still in her lap. She wasn't sure why it hurt so much. Was this the man he truly was? Would he reject her at the merest hint of something or someone else?

She wanted to run back to her father, but she didn't seem to have the energy to move, the energy to continue. It was as though something faltered in her chest. She closed her eyes, trying to imagine Ana and that dark look when she had told her to stop shining. The creature who watched her so closely in the tavern, who could see more of what she was than she seemed to be able to.

But she didn't feel very special right then, didn't feel as though she was someone who could light any space. Was she meant to be here, with this man at this time? Was this what she was shining for, or would it lead her down a different path?

She had seen Ed as a man long before it had been acknowledged that the boy king was no longer a boy. And behind her closed eyes, trying to calm her breathing, she tried to remember the young man appearing from between the trees, the shiny sword cutting into the men and the injury he sustained trying to help her, help them. He had seemed far more like a king then than just now, standing amidst the green field trying to assert he was King.

For the first time, Belle didn't know what she wanted. But then, as she thought of him sitting against a tree, his chest exposed and a deep wound in his shoulder, she did. Belle was sure of the man he had been and, whether he wanted her to be a part of that or not, she would help him. She would find a way to shine her light against Ana's creatures.

A warm hand took hers and squeezed her fingers tight, and she opened her eyes to the sunny day just as he pressed his lips to hers. Belle blinked back her uncertainty.

"This is all my fault," he whispered, moving away from her only a little as he moved his other hand around her face. "I wanted an easy way to regain my crown, and it wasn't possible."

Belle gulped down whatever response she might have made as he kissed her again.

"Dray is right," he murmured as he pulled her close against his chest. "Blood will have to be spilled." His lips moved to hers again, almost desperate, as though he might lose her too. His desperation overwhelmed every other feeling.

She shook her head and tried to pull back, wanting to find herself in the turmoil around her.

"Whatever happens, I want you there. I need you beside me."

She blinked at him then, trying to see through the too-bright sunlight that was obscuring him from view.

"I told Dray long ago," he whispered in her ear, holding her even tighter, "but I don't think I told you."

Belle could see nothing but light, nothing but golden sunshine, blinding her to the world.

No one moved. It was as though the world had stopped around her, frozen from fear of what might have been, what she might be truly capable of. Of what Ana might do to use her.

"Belle?"

She blinked as the light faded and Ed came into focus. The uncertainty that had overwhelmed her dissipated with the light. She sucked in a sob, unsure what it meant, unsure what she was. She clung to the man before her who held her tight, but not as he had before, not as though he wouldn't share her with the world, but as he might hold a child to comfort them, and she cried all the more.

"I love you," he whispered into her hair. She wrapped her hands in his shirt as though she couldn't let him go.

Barlow stood beneath the trees and looked into the empty branches. It wasn't that the forest people were hiding; they had disappeared completely. There was no sign of them at all.

"Hello there!" he called again, and then one of the men with him rested a hand on his shoulder.

"Now what do we do?" one of the others asked.

"Did the shadows beat us here?" Barlow asked.

"They can't reach us here. You know that—you saw that."

"Can we be sure?" Barlow asked. He wasn't very trusting of what he thought he saw anymore.

"At least we know the king is not here."

"I doubted he would come," Barlow said, heading for the door that led up to the village in the trees. It creaked open, reminding him how quiet it was in the forest. There was nothing here at all. The staircase inside the tree was dark as he moved quickly up the steps, running his hand along the carved wall.

He blinked into the light on the walkway and travelled along it into a large room set in the trees. It took him a moment to take in the large space, but there was no sign of life. It was neat and tidy, as though it had all been packed away and the owners were just in another room. He went back out to the walkway and peered down at the men below. "Search the entire place."

They nodded and entered the same stairway.

"That won't be necessary," a voice called from the trees. Barlow stopped and looked around. It was both strange and comforting, like the wind through the leaves.

"Why not?" he asked back.

A man appeared in the clearing below. He wore leather pants, but his tanned chest was bare, and his long black hair hung below his shoulders. He stood silently watching Barlow. The other soldiers had stopped along the other walkway.

"They are gone."

"Where?" one of the others asked.

"They fear the queen's power."

"Don't we all?" Barlow murmured.

"Are you King's Men?" the man asked.

Barlow nodded, unsure exactly what he was now. He thought the new queen might refer to them as something very different, but they weren't her soldiers; she had the shadows for that.

"Who are you?" he called back.

"Eilke," the man said. "I am a friend to the king and his soldier."

"Dray?"

The man bowed his head. Barlow headed back down to the clearing to find the man waiting in the same place for him, and the other soldiers emerged from the tree not far behind him.

"You were here?"

"They chose to travel with the women. I showed them the way."

"Was the blond woman a tribute?" one of the soldiers asked.

Eilke looked his way and blinked, but he didn't answer. No matter what Belle had been, she was the king's now, and it did not help them to start gossip. Although if she had been a tribute, perhaps the regent might not have married the forest girl.

"The people here, they have learnt of the queen and what she has done." Barlow said.

Eilke bowed his head again, and Barlow thought he saw pointed ears appear through the man's hair. He took a step forward. "Are you of the trees?" he asked carefully.

"I am Near," he said.

"Near?" one of the others asked, and his companion elbowed him, whispering something. "Near Folk," he choked. "They are myth."

"So many believe," Eilke said.

"Did the king stay with you in the forest?" Barlow asked.

"He is not here," Eilke said, turning back for the trees.

"Do you know where he might be?"

The man continued to walk.

"Can the shadows penetrate the forest?"

"No more," he said, still walking away.

"Can we stay?" Barlow called after him.

He stopped then and turned back to them.

"She can see it all, sense it all," Barlow said. "No thought is private. I don't think she can see us here or know what we do."

"They have travelled closer to our village," Eilke said, turning back to the trees. "You may join us."

They looked between each other and then back at the horses as the man disappeared between the trees.

As they led their horses through the trees, Barlow wondered more than once if following the Near man was a good idea. The lack of animals and birds was somewhat unsettling, and he was sure there should be more creatures living amongst the trees.

But as the light dimmed beneath the thick canopy, he was surprised that they could hear people ahead of them. And then through the trees they found a large number of people camped around a bonfire.

"This is your village?" one of the others asked.

"This is the camp of the forest people. Our village is beyond the trees."

"Can you help us?"

"You must find a way to help yourselves, and we will see what is required of us."

"The queen is not just a threat to us. She is a threat to the entire kingdom."

"Perhaps," Eilke said, disappearing.

Barlow let out a sigh, and the Lord of Near Forest stalked towards them. He squared his shoulders and tried not to put his hand to his sword.

"Has that witch sent you?" the lord demanded.

"Not exactly," Barlow murmured, looking between the trees the Near man had disappeared between.

"I will not give her what is mine," the lord growled. Barlow turned and took in the young man, oozing confidence.

"I think she could take whatever she wanted," he said. "It is very hard to escape her. She will do what she will do. And she can find her way into the mind of any man she chooses."

"She killed my sister," he snapped.

"She has killed even more than her. Or turned them into her creatures."

The lord shivered and then turned to look back over the people. "She doesn't seem to be able to reach us here."

"There is something of the forest that keeps you safe," Barlow said.

"The Near Folk have the trees."

Barlow studied the man, trying to determine his strange turn of phrase.

"The trees are not happy where we live. Long ago," the lord said, calmer now, a different man from the one Barlow had seen in the capital, "our people adjusted the trees so that we could live in the canopy. The trees continue to grow, but they were injured by the magic, and the Near Folk cannot protect us as well there."

"That is why you are staying here?"

"The trees protect us, no matter what our ancestors did. We are of the forest, and the forest looks after its own."

Barlow looked at the groups of people around the clearing and saw some bags of goods, clothing maybe. Women chattered, children ran around, and the men were relaxed although watchful.

"Have you seen any creatures?"

"We have seen them by the forest edges. We are in the heart here, and they cannot reach us."

Barlow breathed for what felt like the first time. How long had he been protecting himself— trying not to think of a way out of this, a way to destroy the queen? Now there was no threat. But if he didn't return to the capital, didn't prove he was trying to do as he was told, he didn't know what that would mean for his future or the men he had left behind.

"We need the king," he murmured.

"The boy might be our only hope," the lord admitted.

Barlow looked at him seriously. "I thought you didn't care for the king."

"I was trying to assert an authority I did not have, and I did not fully appreciate what he was. Nor what it would mean for the kingdom and the forest. My sister had said something about the regent, that he had controlled all the kingdom, not just a little bit of it. I could have slapped her to the floor had she not been in such a position. She was right. The king's place is to watch over the whole kingdom. Now that witch sits on the throne, controlling every corner of the world we know. But she is doing more than demanding loyalty, and she would see us all in darkness rather than prosperity. He might have been a boy, but I should have supported the king." The man sighed and looked down.

Barlow thought it must have taken a lot to admit such a thing, and he wondered if it was just for his benefit or if the man had fully understood his mistake.

"We thought the witch was supporting the king, working to put him back on the throne."

"The story is that he gave her the crown."

Barlow sighed. It was one of the reasons the people hadn't stood against her sooner. They believed the king had handed her what should have been his. And they wondered whether he should rule if he had been prepared to give it away so easily, and not in a way that would benefit them. He was supposed to put the people first.

The young lord sighed and ran his fingers though his hair. "It doesn't really matter now, does it? Not what I thought or what he wanted. The woman is in control, and she will do whatever she wants. With those creatures, there is no way to stop her." He didn't sound panicked; in fact, he sounded too calm. And Barlow understood to some extent why that would be.

"We are safe here," he said.

"And we will remain so. We might have to hide for a time, but the forest will protect us."

"It might not be long before others realise the same."

The lord looked at him as though taking his measure. "I will do what I have to do to protect my people," he said.

"And the rest of the kingdom?"

The man laughed, and Barlow took a small step back. "We have never been truly one. A king long ago forced others to bend to his rule. And they have been demanding proof of that loyalty ever since. We are still provinces, each trying to keep our little part of the world alive."

"Do you think now is the time to be vying for the throne?"

The man laughed all the harder. "I don't think anyone will be that stupid," he spat, anger suddenly apparent in his words. "Each lord will do what he can to protect his people. The rest can look after themselves."

"But the other provinces don't have the forest to protect them."

"If they want to survive, they will find a way."

Barlow studied the man before him, unsure if he was mad or just doing what he could to survive.

"You may stay," he said to them, then turned and returned to the people.

"It isn't like we have a choice," one of his soldiers said behind him.

# 7

Ana watched the woman bent over her desk, the wind blowing through her blond hair and through the papers weighted beneath her. It felt like years since she had stood in this room, and at the same time as though it were only yesterday she had stood on the Walk, Dray's hand tight around hers.

She shook the idea away as she stepped out of the round opening in the wall. As with many other aspects of her life, she no longer feared the fall. She walked slowly to the very edge of the Walk and peered down at the world so far beneath her.

She could hear the waves crashing on the rocks, although the sea spray and fog prevented her from seeing what she knew lay there waiting. If she fell now, her shadows would save her. Her own magic would be enough to prevent her death. She was reminded of the mage, thinking he could live forever.

*You will. If not here, in the beyond.*

Ana turned back to look into the room, reminded of a dream she'd had so many times of the people watching her fall and the dragon hidden in the room. He hadn't been there at the time, yet he had heard her call.

The woman at the desk, usually so apathetic to the world around her, stood. Her body was rigid, her hands grasped the desk before her, and Ana could not only see, but feel the fear in her shaking hands.

"Aunt," she said, walking back into the room.

"Ana?" the woman stammered. "How did you…?" She froze as Ana moved across the room in a blink.

"It appears I have more of my mother than I understood." Ana held her hands out as the woman looked her over. "And I have more power than you would have liked me to have." She looked at the teacup sitting on the desk. With a quick wave of her fingers, it flew across the room and shattered against the far wall. "But then you knew that too, didn't you, Aunt? It was why you sold me to the mage."

"I wanted more for you," the woman said, her confidence returning, although Ana could still sense the underlying fear.

"You wanted me gone," Ana hissed, allowing the darkness to fill her voice.

Her aunt staggered back and sat heavily in the chair.

Ana pointed a finger and raised it to the ceiling, lifting the woman from the chair. "You may not have heard, Aunt, but I am Queen. I am Majesty of this kingdom, this world. There is protocol; there is fealty. Curtsy," she demanded, and the woman dropped into a shallow curtsy.

"Is that all you have? I would have thought you could show more respect for a niece you denied for so long. I wonder…" Ana said, smiling as the woman dropped lower.

"What do you wonder, Majesty?" the woman asked, her voice soft, her eyes downcast. Ana breathed in the joy of the moment.

"If I should leave you here."

She looked up sharply, and Ana waved a hand. The woman slid across the room as Ana appeared in the chair behind the desk. She looked over the array of papers and then towards the opening to the Walk. The sense of power within the room was comforting, and she looked at the woman standing beside the desk.

"Family should stick together," she said sweetly, looking over the aunt she hadn't known and seeing the mother she had only seen in dreams. "You could return with me to the capital."

"Who would take care of the province?"

"I could leave one of my children," Ana said, raising a hand. One of her children appeared before her, bowing awkwardly. "Ruth," she said, and the child blinked. "You could hold my aunt's place for a little while."

The creature took in the woman before turning into a perfect copy. The Lord of Sheer Rock stumbled backwards.

"Beware of the Walk," Ana warned, and the woman turned to take her in, glancing between the two of them and the opening to the Walk.

"What do you want?" she stammered.

"What did you do to my mother?"

"Mariela? Nothing."

"She left us, and she was lost to the world. Separated," Ana said, the word burning through her.

"She needed to be with the mage, I thought. I don't know. She returned here with a husband and gave birth to you not long after. And then she was gone."

"Why did you think she had gone to the mage?"

"She had gone to him, apprenticed with him when I took over for our father."

"Was it your place?"

"I was the eldest child."

"Were you?" Ana asked, feeling the lie.

"It is documented. If she were the eldest, Father would have made her stay. Her place would have been here."

"But she had magic. Magic is not seen in the line. Magic is to be banished."

"He didn't know what to do with her," the woman said, her voice loud.

"You are not blameless," Ana said, standing slowly.

"She didn't want it. When she returned, she was only interested in her family." The woman stepped closer to Ana, wanting her to believe it.

Ana could feel the woman's jealousy for what her sister had. No matter what power she had as a lord, it was not the same.

"And you destroyed her family too."

"She left," the woman implored. Desperation leached into the room. Ana breathed it in. It would be so easy to kill this woman, destroy her as she had destroyed her own family. But it wasn't what Ana needed now. She needed to know where her mother had gone, what she had done and how she had been separated from her magic.

"Don't kill me," the lord whimpered, dropping to the floor. "Please, Ana."

Ruth returned to her shadow form and hissed angrily at the woman, who cowered away as large tears tracked down her cheeks. "Majesty," the child hissed. "You are nothing. She no longer needs that name. It is Majesty."

"Forgive me, Majesty," the woman begged, climbing to her knees to bow down.

"I will give you an opportunity to show what you are worth on these islands. To prove you are strong enough to be Lord."

"Anything," the woman said, bowing her head down to the floor.

Ana called the shadows forward, and the woman looked around the room. The overwhelming fear strengthened Ana all the more. She nodded just once. The woman screamed as a shadow moved over her, and she was gone.

Almost immediately it reappeared before her, bowing low, looking like the woman she had run from so long ago.

"Prove yourself or die," Ana said.

The woman nodded awkwardly and sat down at the desk. Ana replaced the cup of tea on the edge of the desk, although the fragments of the previous cup remained embedded in the wall.

Ana looked around the small cottage she had called home for so long. A narrow bed still sat at either end of the space; the one with a screen across it had been her parents'. The small table sat in the middle of the cottage, and the fireplace with pots hanging over it was just as she had left it the morning she had gone to work and never returned. The entire cottage was covered in a thick layer of dust, other than a place by a chair that had been pulled out by the table.

She wanted something from this place, some indication as to who her mother had been and why she had disappeared as she had. Not because Ana missed her—not because Ana felt anything lacking. She didn't now. There was no nostalgia, no anger at the woman she had just consumed who had murdered her father and tried to do the same to her.

She needed to know what had happened to the woman who contained the same magic she had, and whether they had been separated. She needed to understand how the shadows had become trapped in a book. But although the shadow was strong, and the creature it had become a worthy servant, it might be something very different to separate a queen.

Ana looked around the lonely space. Then, as she was sure

someone was at the latch, she blinked from the little cottage to the secret room in the capital that the shadows had claimed as her mother's. Looking around the space, Ana wondered if her mother had been captive there rather than hiding.

They were very different women. No matter what the mage thought he could do to her, he had no way to get close, no magic strong enough to defeat her. Even the little girl with the light could have been something, but she didn't know what she was, didn't know what she could do with it, and in the end she was no threat to Ana. To others maybe, but not her. Not a queen of both worlds.

Ana stepped up to one of the narrow windows and looked down over the world below. There was only one who might determine what she could do with the light, what damage that might do. But Belle had run far away with her king and the soldier.

She didn't understand what she had, didn't fully realise when she shone, although never enough to do any damage. Ana doubted she would work it out.

Ana paced the small room, looking over the few items and finding nothing to connect her or her mother to any of it. She growled out her frustrations and reappeared in the throne room, making the guards by the door jump and the child lurking before the throne look up.

"Where have you been?" Ana asked the child, but it only glanced her way and then looked back to the throne. "Do you have the same idea that someone else will win it if I'm not sitting in it at all times?"

"Let me hunt out the boy," hissed the child, once a major.

"Is there really a need?" Ana asked, looking the child over. "I want him gone, but he will resurface on his own soon enough."

"You were not as confident when you sent the soldiers out into the world."

"They were exhausting, trying to formulate a plan to remove me when I knew their every action."

"So you send them where we cannot reach them?"

"You would dare question me?" she growled, and the man at the door flinched.

"You are clouded when it comes to the boy. He should have been killed the moment he handed you the crown."

"It wasn't necessary. He is no threat. It gives the people a little hope that I can then crush. I enjoy their disappointment and fear." Ana licked her lips, tasting the faint fear in the air from the soldier by the door. She could really scare him and have more, but there was a fine line with these weak ones. She had killed some by scaring them too much, particularly the older ones. She wondered if they ever would have survived a battle.

"Allow me," the child hissed.

"There are others I have sent. Others will find him and tell me what he does. For now, he hides. Enough!" she snapped, making the soldier jump even further as she sensed the continuing debate within the child. "There are other matters to discuss. I will leave you here to watch over the throne that too many of you fear will be lost if I leave the room. I have somewhere to be."

"Majesty," hissed the child, the words accompanied by an awkward bow.

She blinked from the room, feeling fear and relief flood the soldier with uncertainty as to when she would return. She breathed in the power of the beyond, the shadows thick and comforting. Although she was not as troubled by her time in the world she wanted to make her own, she felt a disconnect here, as though she didn't understand it all.

*This is a bad idea.*

"Truly?"

*We are something very different. We cannot be separated.*

"I need to be sure. She was, at some stage, separated from her magic, and I need to know how it was done."

Ana could feel the shadows within the room, the darkness that strengthened her, and yet she had been unable to move beyond the room. She rarely visited since she had become Queen, and now it felt different, not quite as satiating as it had been before. She walked slowly around the small table, then to the bed. The soft comfort called to her, and yet she ignored it and walked around it.

The room beyond disappeared as it had before, and although she could sense the world beyond, she couldn't see it. "We are Queen," she whispered. She had been able to conjure whatever she wanted in this space previously, although she hadn't wanted for much.

Ana stepped into the shadows at the edges of the room and walked into the darkness. As when she had tried before, nothing happened and she got no further. She growled with frustration, the sound echoing through the fog surrounding her. Why couldn't she see beyond this space?

*It is not for us.*

"But it was. We are Queen of both worlds."

*It is not as easy as you wish it to be. I was born with you. I am Queen of this world, and yet it has been too long since I was here.*

"I?" Ana questioned. "It has always been *we*. No matter what you were before, we are Queen now of two worlds. We have been one always."

*Not always.*

"The shadows know me. They recognised us long before I fully understood what we were."

*You cannot destroy the shadows. No matter what you try, they will always reform.*

"We have linked the worlds. Our children move between them. And yet I cannot."

*We are not as strong as we hoped.*

"I will not accept that." Ana returned to the throne room. The lights of the day dimmed as a soldier moved through the room lighting sparsely spaced torches. "Leave them," she growled.

He bowed quickly and was gone.

"Must I be shadow to move through the world?" she wondered aloud.

*The children are more shadow than alive, more of my world than yours, more of that world than this. It is the way it has always been.*

"I am the same," Ana huffed, sitting on the cold stone of the throne and breathing in the power she had, the strength the dark gave her, even here.

*We were never the same. Stronger and yet weaker, connected and yet unable to cross beyond.*

Ana sighed, wondering what others had done to try to reach the world she wanted so desperately, although she hadn't wanted it until this moment. She had been content with this world; this was the world she had wanted from the beginning. This was hers to rule, and rule she would. But the niggling fear grew at the back of her mind that there was more, more to endanger her, more that she should have.

She stood quickly and blinked from the room before anyone

could tell her she shouldn't. Who would dare to threaten her place on the throne? Even if they—the boy, the soldier, the little girl who glowed—managed to find a way to rise against her, they didn't have the strength. They didn't have the soldiers she did. She would destroy them in a heartbeat, and they knew as much. It was why they stayed away.

Although she would rather know where they were and what they were doing, which was why she had sent her children after them.

She stepped up to the narrow window in the room that had been her mother's. Closing her eyes and reaching out her senses through the wall, she was reminded of the ice cells of the mage. The apparent lack of doors although the mage had opened them easily enough. Perhaps this was the same. But there was no opening she could sense, nothing but solid walls. She wondered who had created such a room, who had first hidden away here, or hidden someone else.

It had once seemed like a good place to hide the soldier, although she couldn't understand such a need now. He was just a man, any connection lost. Any understanding gone. She remembered all that had happened before—his strong hand around her wrist, his pulling her far from the world she knew and getting lost in the mountains, her searching for him when she'd been pulled far away—but none of it contained any emotion. She understood what she had felt at the time, mostly fear, but she no longer had the same feelings. It was as though she watched someone else's life.

All Ana wanted was to be Queen, to rule over her kingdom, to be the queen she had wanted to be once she knew it was her destiny and not the boy's to sit on the throne. She ran her hand over the narrow mantle, the thick dust collecting under her fingers. It could stay as it was. She didn't need this space; she needed to work out how to rule this nation, not just enjoy the fear she raised in its people. She needed more. She needed to show them she was more.

She blinked back to the throne room and waved the soldier forward. He hesitated for only a moment and then took a step forward.

"Who did the regent talk with?"

"Majesty?" The man's voice shook more than his body did.

"Who came to see him here?"

"Umm, people from the kingdom, with grievances or wanting something, those with news they thought he should know."

"The province lords?"

He shook his head.

"He wasn't interested," she said slowly, sitting down. But should he have shown that he cared even if he didn't? She tapped her fingernails on the armrest.

"What would you like me to do?"

He looked a little more confident, Ana thought as she looked him over. Perhaps he thought he might get a chance to leave the room. "Send for the lords."

"All of them?"

She tapped her finger again, the sound echoing through the room. She knew where her aunt was, and the Lord of Edge Mountains was already gone. "The south," she said.

"South?" he asked with a gulp, his fear starting to increase. As much as she enjoyed it, she took a slow breath and smiled. He took a step back.

Ana cleared her throat. "The provinces to the south, the grasslands, desert. Do the marshes have a lord?"

He nodded once.

"Them. I want to see them."

He bowed low, and Ana noted just how fluid the movement, despite his uncertainty. Then he raced for the door. He paused and turned back slowly.

"Do you want me to send another?" he asked.

She shook her head. She could look after herself, despite what her children thought was best.

*Queens deserve men to watch over them. It is more status than fear.*

Ana sighed and looked out over the empty room. She didn't miss the people, the odd times she had watched this room filled with people vying for a man's attention. But she wanted to direct more of what occurred in her world. If she couldn't reach the other, she would ensure this was completely hers.

*What if they will not follow?*

"Then I help them, as I did my aunt."

# 8

Ed stood at the end of the table and looked over those sitting around it. He wasn't sure how to ask them for what he needed. He knew it was too much to ask of them, but he had no one else. This was his family, and they did what they could for each other.

"Just spit it out," Phillip said without looking up from his plate.

"We need to fight Ana. We need to stand up to her to save the kingdom."

Stoney silence met him. He locked eyes with Dray, who nodded once.

"We knew this was the only way."

"But how do we get close without her creatures killing us?" Forest asked. "They are everywhere, and although they have left us alone, she won't hold back as soon as you are seen as a threat. She isn't the same woman…"

Ed held up a hand. He knew as much; he had seen as much in the throne room. And he didn't need to be told what he already knew.

"It is going to be bloody," Dray murmured. "We will be fighting the people you want to protect, whether they want to fight you or not. And we hardly have a force."

"Maybe we could gather an army on the way, those willing to fight."

"How do we make it that far?" Forest asked.

Ed gulped down the fear rising in his chest. He had no idea. He only knew it had to be done. "She only grows stronger."

Dray looked across the table at Belle, who looked up too. Ed still felt a twinge of jealousy when they were together or shared a look. The day before, Ed had reacted badly to finding her with Dray, having mistaken what they were to each other, and then nearly lost her in trying to hold on to her. She had been so upset, and for a moment he thought she had glowed, but it had been fleeting and he wasn't sure. He had been too busy trying to hold her.

Forest cleared his throat, and Ed realised he had been staring at Belle, who glowed pink from the attention. "It will be hard enough to reach Near Forest, let alone the capital, without being found by those creatures. But if we try to drag an army with us, we are doomed."

"We might not have to take the fight to her," Dray said. Ed nodded for him to continue. "If we can reach the forest and find support there, it might be that once we have the numbers that is all we need."

"She will come to us?"

"Perhaps. If we are ready, we could take them on wherever we meet."

"Ready?" Forest asked. "Have you lost your mind?"

The room turned its focus on him.

"Even if she didn't have an army, if she only had a few of those creatures, we wouldn't be able to fight them."

"Light," Belle murmured. She looked around the group. "The dragons. Once we need help, they will come. They will help, and those creatures against two dragons don't stand a chance."

"Are you sure?" Forest asked. "Or are you guessing? I don't want to risk my daughter on a guess. And I fear we have only seen part of what Ana is capable of."

"If she could hunt us out and destroy us, she would have."

"I think whatever link she had to us is broken," Dray said softly, and Belle gave him a sympathetic look across the table. "She won't see us until we make ourselves known."

"It is too big a risk." Forest pushed up from the table and left the small cottage. Phillip watched him go while Dray looked at the table.

"I can't hide here forever. One way or another she will find us and kill us. We have to remove her first."

Dray gulped slowly and nodded.

Ed wanted to say something reassuring, but he wasn't sure what.

"I know she is already gone," Dray murmured, pushing up from the table and walking towards the door. He stopped in the doorway and turned back. "If we can make it to the forest, we might have a chance."

Ed nodded thanks and sat down on the end of the bench seat.

Phillip had taken Belle's hand.

"I would leave her if I could," Ed murmured.

"But you can't do this without her," Phillip said. "Whatever gift she has might be your only chance."

"I don't have a gift," Belle said, squeezing his hand in return. "Or if I do, I can't find it. I don't know how to make it work."

"We can try." Ed smiled although it was hard. "Phillip, sir, before we go I would like to talk to you about something important."

"I might have been good with an axe, lad, but this is not for me."

"That's not..." He looked at Belle, who gave him a quizzical look and then blushed brightly. For a moment Ed thought he saw a glow surrounding her, but he wondered if he just wanted to see it.

Phillip looked at her and then back to Ed before standing from the table. Ed stood opposite, his chest tight, finding it strangely hard to breathe. Phillip nodded slowly. "Do you promise to look after her, Your Majesty?"

"With everything I have," Ed said in a rush.

"Then you have my blessing."

Ed bowed low before Phillip, who laughed. When he straightened, he and Belle were alone in the dim light of the cottage. "This is what you want too?" he asked, fear taking hold of his chest again.

She nodded. The smile she gave him lit up the world around her.

Dray watched Belle as they moved along the narrow tracks that led through the tall green grasses. He glanced up at the seeded tops swaying in the breeze well above his head. The world beyond the track they followed was impossible to see. Dray had not really visited this part of the world in his earlier days, and he had an understanding that the grasslands were filled with farmers and crops, but he had no idea it was hidden behind the tall stalks.

Phillip had assured him that the world looked different when the crops were harvested, but he could barely comprehend how much ground the crops covered when he couldn't see beyond the current field.

Belle continued on, Ed a step behind while Forest lingered at the back of the group. It was almost as though he didn't want to be there, and it was strange being led by the girl who not so long ago seemed to cling to the king in fear.

She stopped and turned to face him, her blue eyes meeting his. It was almost as though she could sense him when she opened her mouth to say something and then closed it.

"What is it?" Ed asked, stepping forward to take her hand. She shook her head, but her focus remained on Dray.

Forest cleared his throat as he stopped beside Dray. "There is something so alike in them," he murmured.

"And yet very different," Dray added.

Ed shot a confused look in their direction, and Belle turned back to the path and continued.

"She does have some skill," Forest said.

"But not like Ana did; it is something different. And I don't think she has fully worked it out yet."

"No," Belle called back. "I haven't."

Dray smiled, despite the uncomfortable look the king turned his way. She would work it out when the time came. Of all the months they had spent at the farm, it was only in the last little while that she had started to talk to him, started to talk to anyone. She had spent so long looking in to determine what she was. And she would, when the time was right, Dray was certain. She would work out what she was and how she could protect those around her she cared for. Ed. She was another woman focused on Ed, but Dray didn't mind. He too was here for the king, to keep him safe and try, again, to find a way for him to regain his crown.

"Do you think of her?" Forest asked after some time walking in silence. The question made Dray look around as though she might be near, or one of her creatures. It was too much of a risk to head out as they had and, try as he might to find a way for them not to think about who they were or what they were doing, it was impossible. If her creatures really could read people, they would soon be discovered.

"She isn't what she was," Dray said, taking in the man beside him after searching the surrounding area. He was sure for a moment he could hear someone or something amongst the tall stalks that edged the track, but it might have only been the wind, or his imagination.

Master Forest nodded. "I miss her too," he murmured, walking ahead to catch up with Ed, and Dray felt his feet dragging. He had spent so much time thinking about what she had meant to him, what he had thought he had wanted from her, followed by confusion when she had visited him in his dreams.

And then his dreams had changed, and she had admitted to him that she no longer dreamt. He wondered if that meant she no longer dreamt of him, or if she no longer dreamt at all. She had seen so many things in her dreams, even when they had crossed the mountains. His heart raced at the memory of the night he couldn't wake her, how afraid he had been, how he had taken her in his arms and run, finding Ende and a boy king.

Might the world have been different if they had stayed in the mountains? Stayed lost? He sighed and hurried to catch the others as they started around a curve in the road. If they got too far ahead, he would lose sight of them amidst the grass. He wasn't sure what he could do if he did lose them.

Being lost in the mountains or the grass wasn't going to fix anything now, and it wouldn't have saved Ana. She was what she was, and she might have been that before he had the chance to know her. She had lived a whole life before they had met, and she might have continued down the same path whether he was there or not.

He wondered then what she might have been to the sword master. He had kept her close, watched over her. What of the time they had spent together, the conversations they would have had? Dray didn't feel jealous, although he thought he should. It was time lost, time he could have had with her before she was lost.

Dray ran his fingers through his hair and looked up to see Belle staring at him again, and he nodded once. He couldn't grieve forever. He had been distracted enough when Ana had visited him in his sleep. Now that she was gone, he couldn't behave the same way. There was even more at stake.

"Someone is coming," Belle whispered.

Ed looked into the sky while Dray turned to look behind him, all three of them having drawn their swords.

"Who is it?" Dray asked.

"Can you see someone?" Ed asked, and Dray shook his head.

They turned back to Belle, who looked down at the gravel at her feet, her hands clenched before her.

"Do we hide, run or fight?" Dray asked her, and she raised her eyes slowly.

"Run," she whispered.

She took Ed's hand and pulled him along the path. Dray followed not far behind the sword master. He could sense something behind them but not what it was, and the continued fast pace of the girl in the lead pushed him on. Shadows would find them no matter where they went, but he couldn't guess what or who else it might be.

Belle stopped suddenly, pulling Ed to a sharp halt as he ran past her, his hand still tight around hers. "Hide," she said, looking directly at Dray.

He nodded, and they looked to the tall stalks surrounding them.

Then Dray looked at Ed, who hadn't quite mastered moving through the stalks without pushing them all down. Belle sucked in a deep breath and closed her eyes.

Dray nodded once and tapped her on the shoulder. She turned without looking at him and disappeared into the grass, the sword master following. Dray grimaced at the king. "Forgive me," he muttered as he picked the boy up, realising quickly that he was more a man. He opened his mouth to protest but thought better of it. Dray pushed into the grass, hoping the extra weight didn't damage the slender stalks he moved between.

He moved straight through, not pausing, not looking for a sign of Belle. And after several minutes and Dray shifting the king to his back, they reached a small cottage. It was similar to the one they had been staying in, although it had clearly been abandoned long ago. The door was hanging off, part of the roof had fallen in and the paled wood had started to rot away.

Once inside, Dray lowered the king and Belle nodded her head once.

"You knew this was here?" Ed asked.

"Everyone who grew up around here knows this is here. It was abandoned long ago when the old couple died, leaving no children. The neighbouring farms slowly spread out their crops to take over the empty fields.

"No one took it over?" Forest asked.

"It was said to be haunted," she said, a smile lighting up her face.

"What if they follow us?"

She shook her head.

"Do you know what was following us?"

"I'm not sure if they were following or just happened to be on the same path."

"What did you sense?" Dray asked.

"Fear, darkness."

"Could it have been her creatures?" Ed asked.

"I don't think they follow the roads," Dray said. "Let's wait here a while before we continue, give whoever it was a chance to pass us by."

"If only I could work out what I am," Belle whispered.

"I have seen you glow," Ed said softly.

"Whatever you are, others have seen it. It will come when you need it," Dray said.

There was a loud bang on the side of the building.

The group looked at each other in the dim light of the room and held their collective breath. Dray, sword still in hand, moved slowly towards the doorway and looked out at the surrounding area. He couldn't see anything. Another bang echoed through the space.

The door creaked loudly and scraped across the step as Dray slowly pushed it outward. "What do you want?" he called into the grass, looking each way, unsure what side of the building they were on and just who they might be.

There was no response.

"Forest," he murmured into the dim room. The man stepped forward. Dray indicated he wait in the doorway, then circled the building slowly. For the first time, he missed Kemp. It had certainly been useful to send the creature out to watch from the shadows. He tried to peer around the building and see if there was any indication of people in the surrounding crops.

And then he was looking at the back of a man dressed as any other farmer might be, but there was something quite different about him. Dray let his sword touch the man's back, and he stiffened before straightening and raising his arms.

"What do you want?"

"I thought I saw Belle Poales."

"What do you want?" Dray asked again, poking the sword a little further into the man's back.

He glanced over his shoulder then. "My father will not appreciate you doing that."

Dray raised his eyebrows.

"I have heard all sorts of things," the young man said as Dray took him in. "I…"

"Does your father know you are out in the fields, scaring people?"

"I wasn't…" Dray poked again. "I am not away from my home much. It was luck only that I was able to come out, and more luck that I saw the beauty for myself. I had heard she had run away."

"You were misled."

"Still seems to have found herself some fancy husband from the capital. Why would they be here?" the man asked.

"Visiting family," Dray said. "Perhaps it is time for you to return to your own."

"They will find me soon enough anyway."

"They?" Dray groaned aloud, cursing himself as a blade was drawn behind him. Several blades. He turned slowly to take in the men who had emerged from the field. They didn't appear to be farmers.

He lowered his sword, and the young man stepped up beside him. "I knew you wouldn't be far behind."

"We never are," one man said. "I wonder why you bother."

"I hear things."

Several of the men looked between each other. The young man grunted.

"You need to spend less time with the serving staff," one man laughed.

"But I like your wife," the young man retorted.

The other man's face darkened.

"You could say you found him too late," Dray suggested, reaching for his sword.

"Tempting, but I doubt the lord would be as forgiving, no matter how annoying the boy is."

"Hey," the young man said. "You can't call me that."

"And we cannot call you Lord until your father dies," the other man spat. "No matter what you want."

Dray hoped these men couldn't hear the whispering from inside the cottage. "Well, no harm done," Dray said. "You can take him home and we can continue on our way."

"Where are you headed to?" asked the man with the sword still outstretched.

"We have friends in the Near Forest."

"That is some distance to cover. You are aware that the queen has men"—he shivered—"stationed all over the kingdom. Are you running from her?"

Dray shook his head slowly. Were these more of her men, or where they trying to warn him?

"You had best come with us," he said. "All of you." He motioned for several of the other men to move around to the door, then realised there were far more of them than he had originally thought.

Dray waited as the others were ushered out of the cottage and into the small clearing at the back. He bowed his head to Ed and sighed. Ed raised a shoulder in response, a show of understanding perhaps.

The young man saw Belle and stepped forward with a grin. She barely looked at him, looking over the other men instead. One man with a sword lowered it and stepped forward.

"Belle?" he asked, almost disbelieving. "I heard you ran away."

She gave him a small smile, which made the lord's son scowl, and nodded slowly. "I was saved," she said, stepping in closer to Ed.

"And what are you doing here?"

"We were being followed. I thought it might be someone the queen had sent, and we hid. We are headed to find friends in Near Forest."

The man looked at Dray and then back again.

"Why would the queen be interested in you?" the lord's son asked. Dray wondered what he would do with the information.

"She has interest in the whole kingdom," Dray said. "She is always watching."

The men looked between themselves.

"Either way," the man said. "You will need to come with us. You too, little lord," the man said, his frustration evident. "I've had enough of chasing you today."

# 9

Ed wondered how long it would take them to work out who he was, and whether it would do any of them any good. Phillip had come to the Lord of the Grassland when Belle had been taken but hadn't been able to talk to him. What stories had they told themselves when the girls of the land had disappeared? The lord had probably done something similar in the past, and if he had helped Phillip regain his daughter, it might have meant more resistance when it came time to produce his own tribute.

He looked at Belle and stretched out his hand, which she took without looking at him. She was focused on the men leading the way along the small path through the grass. He wondered if Ana would even be interested in continuing the tribute, or what she would ask for instead from the lords of the kingdom. He shivered at the idea, and Belle squeezed his hand. The lord's son gave them an odd look. Ed wondered how well he knew Belle.

He turned back to Dray, his expression serious, and tried not to sigh. Despite the man's feelings about anything, Ed knew he would remain with him, protect him. It was his duty, no matter who might have asked it of him previously. Dray gave a subtle shake of his head, and Ed knew it was to keep quiet.

The castle that emerged through the tall grasses was a surprise. Ed wondered that he hadn't noticed any of it before, but then they always seemed to be lost amongst the grass.

"How did they find you?" he asked suddenly. Belle looked confused. "When they stole you for tribute, how did they find you amongst the grass?"

"It was harvest time; the world looked very different."

Ed tried to picture the world bare around him, but he couldn't. The castle was a similar size to the one where they had stayed in the mountains, once the glamour had been removed. They moved through the wide portcullis to find a large open courtyard, and Ed breathed in the space around him. He hadn't realised how hard it was surrounded at all times by tall grasses, but he noticed it now he was free.

The castle itself rose up around three sides of the courtyard, three stories high. Large windows, made up of small panes of glass, looked over the courtyard. As he turned slowly, he saw a man standing at a window.

If Ana sent her shadows, they wouldn't stand a chance. Ed gulped down the sudden fear and followed the men who had directed them here through a large doorway, that almost immediately took them up a wide staircase, which he was sure led to the man who had looked at them from the window.

They continued in silence. As they walked, Ed found himself at the front of the group, Belle's hand still in his, Dray and Forest at his rear. When they entered a long room, Ed noticed the man alone in the space, still looking out the window. He was reminded of the chief of the Near Folk in some ways. This man was older, but there was something strong about him, something that indicated in the way he stood that he was in charge here.

"You will never guess, Father," the young man said, racing forward. Ed had forgotten the young man had been traveling with them.

"You have forgotten who you are," the older man said without turning from the window, his voice sad.

"I have not," the young man spat.

"It no longer matters," the old man murmured, turning and

taking in the group. When he locked eyes with Ed, he sighed.

"She has been here," Ed said. "Or sent her children to deliver her demands."

The man nodded slowly. Ed was relieved to have missed them, but he wasn't so sure they had gone. Dray stepped forward slowly, looking the man over.

"She has not changed me, or taken me," the lord said.

"How can we be sure?" Belle whispered.

Dray chewed on his lip and then sucked in a breath. "Bow to your king," he said, but his voice was soft, not demanding. The man took a step forward, looking at Ed, and then he bowed smoothly before dropping to a knee.

Dray was the first to sigh with relief, and Belle sat on the floor.

"Fetch the lady a chair," the lord said, climbing slowly to his feet. "I apologise for the manner in which you arrive, Your Majesty."

"Father, I think you might have made a mistake," the young man said, staring as a chair was carried closer. Belle was offered a hand by a soldier and Ed, and she wiped hastily at her face.

"What were you doing?" the lord snapped, turning on the young man, who took a step back.

"I just wanted to take a walk," he said.

The lord turned to the men who had escorted them in.

"My lord," one said. "He was near the road that leads north."

The lord glared again at the son. Ed thought it might have been better that he hadn't been present when the queen had sent her children. One smart word and they might have taken him with them. Or left him to spy. Ed stepped forward and looked him over too. "Bow," he demanded.

The boy turned to his father rather than obey and then, at the look on his face, bowed quickly. Although it did not convey any respect, it was a fluid motion. Dray ran his fingers through his hair, and Ed wanted to laugh. They couldn't test everyone they came across or they wouldn't be able to sneak across the kingdom.

"What did she ask for?" Ed asked.

"Loyalty, continued support to ensure the kingdom thrives."

Ed looked at Dray, who raised a shoulder.

"She might want to appear to be the queen she thinks she is," Forest offered.

"You did give her the crown," one of the men behind them said. "Did you not think she would be the ideal ruler for Ilia?"

Ed looked down and sighed. He had given it away, just as Ende had predicted, and the idea made him wonder when Salima would hunt him out again.

"There wasn't much choice," Dray said for him, stepping in closer. "Will you tell her we are here?"

The lord shook his head. "I will do what I need to for the people of the grassland, as I have always done, Your Majesty. And I believe you are still our true king. But until we find a way to remove the witch from the throne, I will do as she directs."

"It will take great numbers," Ed said slowly, and the older man shook his head. "I understand. She is strong, as are her shadow monsters."

"Why are you in the grasslands?" the son asked.

"We were staying with my father," Belle said.

"Hiding," the young man sneered.

"Have you seen what she can do?" Belle asked, standing slowly. Ed reached out a hand to steady her, but she shook him off. "Have you seen her shadows consume people, or the magic she holds?"

The young man scoffed.

"She could destroy you in a heartbeat, and you wouldn't know what took you until she had you killing others on her behalf."

"She controls the monsters, not me," the young man said, too confidently.

"She controls the world, and every shadow within it," his father answered. "And so we will do as she directs." He was firm, and the boy looked at the floor.

"You are not safe if we stay," Ed said. "She has not sought us so far, but it is only a matter of time."

The boy sighed as though he didn't think them anything of consequence. But it was one of the men behind them who stepped forward and bowed his head to the lord. "Are you sure this is the king?" he asked.

The lord smiled for the first time. "I met with his father often; he is the image of the man. So this young man is King Edwin, or…" He looked up at the man. "King Barric was not as faithful to his beautiful bride as the world believed."

The man turned and bowed his head to Ed. "We will leave you to talk," he said, looking at the lord's son.

"It might have been some time since our king has had a decent meal. Tell cook to prepare for guests."

The man bowed again, and the small group of men left. Ed wondered what they might have achieved if they had followed after Belle as Phillip had been so keen to have them do. She might have been saved before she had reached the edge of the grasslands.

"Did she come, or did she send a monster?" Dray asked.

The lord looked him over before he spoke. "A soldier."

Dray looked at Ed, and he could see the concern as to who it might have been.

"I don't think there is any connection with Kemp," Ed tried to assure Dray, although he wasn't as certain of the words as he wanted Dray to believe.

"A major of the King… Queen's Men. But he was not like any major I have seen before."

"Field," Dray growled.

"He appeared in the middle of the room, as though drawn from the shadows themselves." The man looked Ed square in the face.

"We could have taken such a man," the son scoffed.

"You aren't that good with a sword," his father returned. "And he was not a man."

"One of her shadow children," Dray admitted. "We knew him

before. We watched him consumed."

"We have not seen him since, but she has so many now."

"How can you fight against such an army?" the lord asked. "They would convert your allies before you had a chance to reach them."

"It will not be easy," Ed said. "But we have allies with different skills who may be able to prevent such a thing."

"May?" It was the boy who asked the question as he looked at Belle. "You have no idea. Would you drag a woman into battle? As though women could be of any use."

Belle stood slowly. "We are fighting a woman who has taken control of the kingdom. One woman created an army of her own, destroyed her enemies and has grown in strength. I wonder at your fear of taking up a sword against her when she is only a woman."

The young man coloured, but he turned to his father.

"Miss Poales, I appreciate that you have had a difficult time, running away as you did." He held up a hand as she opened her mouth to speak. "You have found good friends here, I see. But the boy is right. Unless you have a magic that could assist, I see little need to send you out to be slaughtered."

"You were happy enough to send me off to be married to some old man, just to please a man who wasn't even king."

"Belle," Ed said softly, unsure how he could reassure her without giving away what she might be to these people.

She sighed and sat back down on the chair.

"Maybe you are a witch as well," the boy said.

It was Dray who leapt forward, making the boy jump. But by the time his hand found his sword, Dray's blade was already at his throat. Ed stepped forward, resting his hand on Dray's shoulder.

Dray sheathed the sword and stepped back immediately, bowing to the lord. "My apologies," he said shortly and then stalked from the room.

Ed turned to Belle, held out his hand and pulled her to her feet. "We have trespassed on your time long enough," he said without making eye contact with the lord. "We appreciate your discretion as to our whereabouts." He turned, taking Belle with him and nodding to Forest, who had remained silent throughout the exchange. They followed Dray's path towards the door.

Once they were back in the courtyard, Ed pulled Belle close. Dray paced back and forth.

"He would be a useful friend," Forest suggested. "Although if Ana has already reached out to the lords, he might not be safe."

"The son certainly isn't," Ed murmured.

"What is she trying to do?" Dray muttered as he continued to pace.

"You can't try to work out what and who she is. She is not a woman anymore." Forest sounded harsh, and it stopped Dray's pacing.

"I know that Ana is gone," he said, his voice soft and scary. "I know that witch is not Ana."

"And yet…"

"And yet nothing. We need to work out what she does so that we can stop her. That is my only concern." He turned on his heel then, the bag of supplies still over his shoulder. Ed wondered at how it didn't slow him down.

"Where are the other supplies?" he asked.

"Left at the cottage," Belle said as they followed Dray out of the castle and back into the thick green grass. Ed longed to be in the castle, eating something hot and not stew.

# 10

The mage stood in the damp building, wondering how his life had reached this stage. For he had always been where he wanted to be. Even as a child, he'd gotten everything he wanted, and that wasn't just because of his skill and the people he could manipulate. He had been born to be something great, better than what he was in this moment. Standing wet, in the doorway of a rundown tavern, hoping it led him in the direction he wanted and out of sight of the shadows. Although the shadows seemed to find him wherever he went and whatever he did.

He wanted to curse the girl. All of them. For none of them had given him what he had hoped. Ana had the strength but, after all, the regent had been correct. His only chance now was to find the boy and hope he would accept his assistance. For the mage had done very little for the boy to trust him. Edwin might have learnt the truth of what had happened to his father, but the regent had taken the blame and suggested he was the one with all the power. Although the mage had assisted, providing a way for the regent to get close to his brother and find a way to kill him.

He sighed. It had been too easy in the end, distracted as Barric was by his wife's death. But then they hadn't really known the truth of that. There were rumours that she had been involved with one of his friends, yet the mage had never seen any proof of it, and despite his relationship with Mariela, she had never shared any such stories with him either.

He had once suspected that the young king had killed her out of jealousy. The clerics had cared for her in those last days, and they would have reported something if her death had been unnatural.

He stepped further into the building, wondering at what lay in the dark and whether he could survive with the witch after him. Although she might think that he was doing as she bid. She had sent him out to find the king after all, but they would know he didn't do it for her.

The pale moonlight showed enough of the room that he could see the fireplace, and he rushed forward and placed his hands in the hearth. It felt dry, even to his damp fingers. He rummaged in his bag to find a small bottle. It clinked against others, and he was glad he had taken the time to gather supplies before heading out into the world.

He poured a few drops of the liquid onto the dry wood and then stoppered it before dropping it back into the bag. The clinking of the bottles within sounded similar to his workshop. He leant forward and breathed slowly over the wood. A small flame jumped to life, moving along the log and then back again before nestling down. The heat of the flames made the mage lean back. He smiled as the shadows of the room shrank back and the bright flames lit up the space around him. There were piles of blankets, tables and chairs stacked together, although there were leaves and debris on the floor as though the door had stood open and the outside world had blown in.

He moved through to the bar and the kitchen beyond to find several windows broken. It wasn't too cold, and he pulled the door closed behind him as he headed back to the main room.

He looked up the stairs but was not tempted to explore. He had somewhere he needed to be. He just needed some time out of the rain and dark. He sat before the fire, crossed his old legs and peered once more into the bag.

He pulled out a tall, slender bottle, removed the stopper, sniffed at it and took a deep swig from it. He coughed as it burned his throat, then took another swig before stoppering the bottle and putting it down before him. Next he pulled out a small scrap of thick black woollen cloth, only the size of his palm. He still was not sure how he had managed to obtain it, for the cloak had been lost and yet he knew it to be hers. He had wondered at the significance. She had worn it, he thought, to hide in the shadows, yet she could do that well enough no matter what she wore.

It meant something. It meant something to her. He sat the square on the floor before him and felt around in the bag for another bottle. He poured a couple of drops of the contents into his hand and pushed his hand down over the material. Putting his other hand over the top, he closed his eyes and thought only of the little witch he had hoped was a mage.

"What are you doing?" he whispered into the room.

He saw the soldier, tall, dark, missing his armour, surrounded by tall grasses. Then the witch came into view. Her green eyes flashed, and the fire went out in the same instant that the vision failed.

He sighed and hoped it was a link to her rather than a window for her to see him. As the fire roared back to life, he lifted the cloth to throw it in but instead curled it into his hand and pushed it back into the bag.

That explained why she had let the boy and his soldier go when she had taken the throne. There was still something there, some feeling she had for them. For the tall, dark-eyed man. He might be able to use that.

The Lord of Near Forest appeared to ensure that everyone had food, including Barlow and his men. Barlow had expected him to be something very different. When he came over to their camp, handing out bread and sitting down amongst them, Barlow was reminded of the sister. She had been more like the lord than she had indicated. Although she had been taken by one of the witch's creatures and then killed by the witch herself, Barlow was sure she was with the regent deliberately. That she had been there for the power.

"I won't talk of her," the man said before Barlow could even open his mouth. "I know you were there. I know you saw her. Whatever she was in the end, it was not my sister. She was not Dahli."

Barlow bowed his head once. "Will you hide away here, or would you help us fight her?"

"Fight her? The queen?" The lord leaned back and laughed, a mad cackle that filled the trees around them and went on for too long. In the silence that followed, he looked at them all as though they were the mad ones. "Did you really think you could find an army amongst the trees?"

Barlow shook his head. "I wasn't sure what we were looking for when we headed out. Sanctuary, perhaps. A way to find the king and end this mess."

The smile had slipped from the young lord's face, and he sighed. "I cannot be what you need me to be, nor give you what you want." He turned back to the people beneath the trees. "They are not soldiers; they are villagers. Perhaps if we asked them to take up arms against some other enemy…" He looked truly defeated when he turned back to Barlow. "There is no way we can fight the witch. She is far too strong, I don't even know what magic she has, let alone the creatures and shadows she commands. Any man who tries to stand against her will be lost. Our only hope is to stay within the protection of the trees. If your king arrives by some miracle, finds his way here from wherever he might be hiding, you can send him out to fight the darkness. But it won't be with any of my people following."

Barlow had nothing he could say as he watched the lord head back to those people he was prepared to do so much to protect. At least by remaining where they were. And he could understand that. They had seen just what she could do; he had witnessed many try to stand against her and lose. He wasn't even sure how she had managed to take the crown from the king, and she claimed he had handed it to her. If the rightful king of Ilia struggled to stand against her, what hope did the people have?

"Will the king come?" a child asked, appearing beside him. He looked up into the girl's hopeful face.

He nodded once and hoped it was true.

"Will he stop the queen and allow us to go home?"

"I'm sure he will have a way," Barlow said. The girl grinned and skipped away.

"You shouldn't have said that," one of the men murmured.

"There has to be some hope," Barlow said, biting into the bread he had been handed by the lord. And maybe the king did have a plan. He had managed to survive this long.

# 11

The child appeared before Ana, bowing even more awkwardly than usual, and for a moment she regretted sending it so far away. But the kingdom was vast. If she was to maintain a hold over it all while remaining within the throne room, as everyone insisted she did, she had to use what she could.

Ana nodded for it to tell her the news.

"The lord will do as directed," the creature hissed.

"The Lord of the Dry."

"An apt name, although the land of the sun would have served as well."

Ana stood slowly and stepped forward, looking over the creature whose head was still bowed before her, taking in the dark skin and the cool it emitted. "You were not hurt." It was not a question.

"It took me longer than I hoped, that is all."

"What did he say?"

"The lord is a woman, an older woman, her hair grey, her fingers gnarled. It is not worth what life she has left to defy you."

Ana smiled and sat back in the throne. "Has she seen any sign of the boy and his friends?"

"No, Majesty, although there was the fleeting thought of a dragon."

"One or two?"

"One, Majesty."

Ana tapped her long nails against the hard stone of the throne arm rest. "What are they up to?" she wondered aloud.

*Finding a way to stop you.* Ana's hand closed tight around the armrest, the stone cracking within her hold. *Trying to find a way.*

If anyone could, it would be one of the dragons. Ende had seen too much of what was to come, long before she had become what she was, before the true nature of her strength had been revealed. She wondered if that was why they had disappeared. If he had known what strength she truly had.

"They are hiding," she announced.

"It matters not, Majesty, for the lord will support you. She is preparing tribute to show her fealty. She will send on the next full moon."

"Truly?" Ana asked, taking in the creature before her as though she hadn't really paid it proper attention. "Sending tribute. I wonder what she feels would show such loyalty to a queen who could take whatever she wanted. What does the desert possess that I would want?"

"I know not, Majesty."

Ana drummed her fingers again, small chips of stone falling away as she tapped.

"The Lord of the Grasslands was compliant," she hummed, "but did not promise me gifts."

The creature before her waited, the light catching its sharp teeth as a long tongue licked over scaley skin, tasting the air.

"Go and ask what he will give me," she demanded. "He may have promised support, but I want proof, like the kings of old. Wait," she said as the creature started to disappear. "Perhaps I should go."

"Majesty." The creature bowed its head as she blinked from the room.

The man before her jumped. She stepped forward, taking him in as he openly stared. He could have been her father, had he lived to such an age; there was something familiar in him and yet unknown.

He threw himself forward from the seat to his knees before her. "Majesty," he whispered. "We are most honoured."

She watched him, head bowed, silver flecks through his dark hair. But something else in the room drew her attention, a young man. Something dark pulled at her, and she turned her gaze to him. He stood for too long, and it was only when she tipped her head to the side that he bowed his head.

The father hissed some instruction, but the boy was too struck with the power before him. A longing called to her.

"Show me what I am owed," she said, her voice low, the darkness of the room drawn to her. The boy dropped to his knees.

She turned back to his father. Regret and embarrassment and fear for what she might do ebbed from him.

"I am here to query my tribute?"

He looked up then, the confusion evident.

"Will you not provide tribute?"

"Only too willingly, Majesty. We will wait for the harvest and then send you our very best."

She closed her eyes and dragged in a breath, tasting the fresh green grasses that surrounded this area of the kingdom, and something else. She turned back to the boy. He focused on what he could gain, not what he could give. He would make an interesting lord. "What would you give?" she asked the boy.

"All that I had, Majesty."

"Truly?"

He nodded wildly and then looked back to the floor. An image of another boy in this very room flashed before her. She took a step closer to the boy. A soldier who was no more, dark and terrifying, a blade held against this boy, against this very wall. He had not worn as well as Ana had expected. He looked unkempt, shaggy.

*He is here.*

Ana nodded once. Or he had been here. She turned her glare

back on the man still kneeling on the floor, his eyes watching her too closely. His fear overwhelming.

"Where is he?" she asked.

"Gone," the lord said too quickly. "I would not help him."

"Where was he going?"

"The forest." He said it reluctantly; he knew he could not hide it from her.

"I could help," the boy offered, too keen.

"I have help," Ana replied without looking at him.

"He will not return, Majesty," the lord murmured.

"Not here, perhaps, but that does not mean he will not return to me." She moved to the window to look out over the tall grasses surrounding the castle. The greens were varied, but still all green.

*We can intercept him. We can destroy him before he reaches the trees.*

Ana wanted that to be true, but she could not sense him. It was both a relief and a disappointment that she did not know where they were at all times. She shook her head.

"I will return," she said, still facing the window when she blinked from the room. The idea that she could appear before them at any time should be enough to ensure they did as they were required. And that wasn't very much. They just had to ensure their part of the kingdom was ticking over, meeting the requirements of keeping the people alive and demonstrating their loyalty to her as Queen.

And she could take it all away anytime she wanted. She sat slowly on the throne and waved the soldiers from the room. Closing her eyes, she focused on the image the boy had shown her. The fear at Dray's fast movements, the cold steel against his neck. He had been protecting Belle, her honour or some such. They were all still working together, but they were no longer working for or against her. They were only trying to survive. And with the kingdom against them, or at least in favour of her, she would soon find a way to eliminate them with very little effort.

❀

Belle squealed as a hand closed around her arm, reaching from the tall grass at the side of the track. She dropped the bag she'd been carrying over her shoulder.

The man who emerged, while maintaining his hold, was one of the lord's men, and one she recognised from earlier.

"You have to come back," he pleaded.

Dray and Ed both drew their swords in the same instant and shared a look. Belle relaxed a little, and the man released his hold.

"The lord wishes to see you again."

"Me?" she asked, but she knew it wasn't her.

"Him," he said with a nod, not indicating the king by name or title.

"What has happened?" Dray asked. Belle wondered what skill or magic he had hidden away, and whether she would ever be able to show or find the magic she had within her.

"The queen called on the lord."

"The witch was here?" Dray stammered. Belle looked at him seriously. Despite all he had lost, and despite his agreeing that Ana was no more, he had always still referred to her as Ana. He had never liked the title of witch. But maybe that was what she was now.

The man bowed his head.

"Did he give us away?" Ed asked.

"He said you were gone."

"And that might be the best idea," Belle said. "She might have left eyes and ears."

Dray nodded slowly. She had watched over them all in some way when she wasn't there, leaving spies in the shadows or using the shadows themselves. The lord had said she had sent one of her creatures earlier. Why would she come herself?

Belle looked back to the man. "She wanted assurance of tribute," he answered, as though he'd understood what she wanted to know.

"I don't think it would be safe for either of us if we followed you."

"Then the lord will come to you," the man said, stepping back and disappearing into the crops. Belle stared after him for a moment, then followed him between the stalks. He had a similar skill in that he didn't give away which way he had gone, didn't leave a trail as Ed did whenever he tried to walk through the crops. And yet she knew where he went. In the dark shadows of the tall stalks that stretched well above her head, Belle came face to face with the older man, who glanced between the stalks and over her shoulder.

Belle turned and looked over her shoulder as well; the others had not followed. "It may not be safe in the shadows," she whispered.

He nodded once and followed as she led back to the small clearing.

He bowed his head to Ed as he emerged, and she noticed that Dray did the same to the lord in return. "What did she want?" Dray asked, all pretence of loyalty gone.

"Tribute," the lord said with as little preamble. Belle smiled despite the setting as she looked between the two; there was something very similar about them.

"Why?" Dray demanded.

"Does it matter?" Ed asked. "Is there method to everything she does?"

"Yes," Dray said matter-of-factly. Belle looked back to the lord, who sighed.

"She seems very sure of herself. Someone else must have offered her something, to appease her. She came to wonder where my tribute was. Once I explained it is only given once the crops are harvested, she appeared to accept that. But whether she will accept what I offer at the time or demand more than the people can give, no one could guess."

Ed nodded slowly as Dray ran his fingers through his hair.

"Does she need the people to survive?" Belle asked, and the man turned his dark eyes on her. "I mean, can she fill the world with her creatures and have that be enough, or does she want to rule over men?"

"We may not know until she decides to tell us herself," the lord said, running his thumb and forefinger through his short, neat beard. "We may not know until she is starving us out," he added softly.

Ed mumbled something as Belle noticed him run his thumb over his palm. Ana had convinced Ed she had a plan to return his crown only to force him into a situation he couldn't escape, and he had given her exactly what she wanted. Belle wondered at what point Ana had decided that she wanted the crown for herself. Was it something she had always wanted, when Ende had seen her so clearly in the mountains as something scary, when she had assured them she was something else? Or had it been more recently, when she was alone in the capital, her magic spinning out of control?

Belle only realised she was stumbling herself when Dray's strong hand took her by the arm and held her steady. She looked into his concerned features. What if she became the same? What if she turned into something or someone else when she worked out what her own magic was? Although it seemed to be something very different, she couldn't get a grip on what that was, how it worked, or how to make it work.

"You are something very different," Dray said softly, his deep voice reverberating along her arm and through her chest.

"But what are you?" she asked before she could stop the thought. He released his hold and stepped back.

"How can I help you?" the lord asked. "How can we stop her?"

Ed shook his head. None of them had any idea of what they were doing.

"We have managed to hide from her. I think she has lost whatever connection she had, and we don't know what we can do next," Belle admitted.

"You suggested force before," the lord said, looking at Dray. "Sheer numbers."

"Where many will die in the attempt for a few to reach her and stop her. I'm not sure how we can do that. I don't know how we can make a difference," Forest said.

Belle turned to him, reminded of his presence and how quiet he had been. He looked at her as though having the same thought. And she hadn't said very much in the last few months. She hadn't been able to work out what she was or how she could help. Now they were trying to drag others into this mess. They needed the help, but they had no idea how they could make any difference.

"I will give you all I have," the lord said.

Belle nodded slowly, understanding that such an amount was far more than he realised.

# 12

Salima sighed and rolled back in the sunshine. It was odd how content she was, how at peace with the world around her, and she wondered at all the stress and worry in her life before this time. How she had searched for Ed, how she had clung to the witch, how she had two fathers. She looked at the dragon snoozing on the rock beside her.

Ende rarely took this form, but as she had rarely released hers, he had given up and joined her. She thought this was in part to try and understand what she thought she was doing. But she didn't need to worry.

"When?" he murmured.

"Soon," she returned, stretching and exposing her belly to the sun.

He looked up then, alert.

She closed her eyes and focused on the sun warming her body. She sensed him change, his footsteps growing closer before he leaned in close. "What do you see?"

Salima held back the shiver that threatened. She saw far more than she had wanted to. Any thought of Ed or Dray or the little group she had come to know formed into a series of visions. She wanted to believe them wrong, imagination. But she knew within her very soul that they were true. That what she saw was to come.

They played out in more and more detail each time. That very morning, she had remembered the dream Ana had dreamt when she had snuggled in close, before her magic had truly returned. A mist, a fight—one that Salima had seen herself many times, only this was from Ana's point of view, from Ana's understanding of what was to come. When she had been Ana.

The fear she felt looking upon Dray's cut face. Salima felt that same fear, understood what it would mean for them all. She turned to the dragon appearing as a man beside her and returned to her own human form. She wrapped her arms around him, drank in his heat, and rested her head against his chest, listening to every strong beat of his heart.

"I cannot live forever," he murmured.

"That is a strange thing to say," she returned, holding him close.

When he didn't reply, she looked up at him as he put his hand to her face. "I see much too, although not as you do."

Salima nodded slowly and returned her ear to his chest. "Tell me of my mother," she whispered.

"I have, often," he returned.

"But I have never had the chance to know her, and you must tell me everything."

"Everything? Do you think I have held back?"

She laughed. "You have told me how much you loved her," she said. "Tell me how she was with Ed."

She felt his loss and disappointment. Her mother had cared for Ed very much, and she would have cared the same for Salima if she had been given the chance. It would take her mind from what was replaying for Salima, until it was time to go to Ed. For the time was coming.

Ana found herself in the small, self-contained room yet again, frustrated with herself that she was using the room, or at least visiting it more and more. She couldn't sense her mother here, for she didn't know the woman. There was no indication that she had lived here other than a shadow once telling Ana it was so.

She turned from the window and looked over the small space again, then closed her eyes and called the child forth.

"Majesty," it hissed, large dark eyes focused only on her.

"Why was she here?"

It bowed its head.

"And yet you were there too."

"I was something very different. Once we were separated, any connection was lost; anything we might have shared was gone."

"Where did she go?" Ana asked, wondering why she would care. Knowing would make no difference to her own rule at this stage. Nor influence how she might act in the future.

"Beyond?" the child hissed, looking over Ana's shoulder. In a heartbeat they were in a different room, surrounded by shadows and hazy edges, a contrast to the room they had been in with its defined edges.

"Where is she?"

"Gone," the child growled, as though it had said so before and couldn't fathom why Ana wasn't understanding. "No more. Like the shadow you destroyed in the throne room."

"Dahli?"

As the child nodded, Ana looked around. Somewhere in this room or space was a fragment of what had been a child such as the one before her.

"The shadow will remain, Majesty."

"Always?"

"It is very hard to kill a shadow. It is what gives us our strength, what drives us forward. It is what stops the men from winning."

Ana blinked up at the creature before her. Someone had won before, separated this shadow from the woman, trapped it within the pages of a book. The woman might have been lost, the creature itself destroyed until its shadow could find another to anchor it to the world.

"Who gave you permission to bond to the girl?"

"She wanted me. Desperately." The child licked at its face with a long tongue. "The world is different now. You have created something different. They cannot separate us, for we are no longer two."

Ana nodded slowly. She had felt such a thing—what had been two was now very clearly one. What would that mean if they tried to separate them now?

"They cannot," the creature hissed, and then it disappeared before being dismissed. Ana would have been angry at such disrespect, but she was preoccupied with where her mother might be, where the remains of the regent's wife could have ended up. She had returned the fragment to the beyond, after all, when she had released it in this very space.

*The child speaks the truth. We cannot be separated.*

Ana wanted so desperately to believe her, yet there was something deep within her, a fear she did not want to admit to, that it would be possible in some way to pull them apart. And she did not know what that would mean for them.

"Why can I visit here and not beyond?"

*This is the beyond.*

"There must be more."

*Must there be more? The dark is all we needed. You bring the dark to the world you knew before. We make it a world for our children.*

Ana looked out beyond the familiar furniture to the shadows she had tried and failed to pass through before. "The world is not as I want it. I want them all bowing down before me."

*They will.*

Ana sighed. At the back of her mind, the boy, the soldier and the little girl who glowed were a danger to that idea. They had no strength, no way to win over her, and yet something caused an uncertainty she did not want.

"He is still a threat," she murmured, blinking back into the empty throne room. The guards were still absent, and no one else had come to see her. No one came to ask her assistance or advice. She was their queen, after all.

"What do the people want of me?" she asked the room.

*Strength, power, certainty.*

"I can provide that. I can provide all they need. And I may need them to want to be here," she thought aloud, moving out into the hallway as a maid scurried away. Those who saw her stopped and bowed their heads as she passed.

A young maid shook with fear when Ana stopped. She tasted the air, trying to curb her excitement. For a moment she wanted to make her a child, to keep her close.

"What, child, do you want?" Ana asked the girl.

Scared eyes looked up and then quickly back to the floor. "Majesty?" The fear increased, and Ana drank it in.

"If another came to the castle, someone claiming it was their right and not mine to sit on the throne, would you follow them?"

"Never, Majesty," the maid said hurriedly, but Ana felt a small glimmer of hope flare in her chest before the girl managed to hide it. She waved her away and continued along her path. There would be others who would appreciate her power, who would stand with her. Perhaps if she gave more to the people, they would follow her into a war.

"You," she called across the courtyard to a young soldier, who froze at her words. His heart also beat quickly. He turned slowly and bowed to her, his fist to his chest, and she tried not to think of another soldier who had once worn shiny armour.

"Majesty," he said, straightening. "How can I assist you?"

She looked him over. There was a touch of excitement mixed with his fear, as though he might become something great, something stronger than what he already was.

"Is that what you would want?"

He stared at her, his blue eyes smiling.

"You can wait. I want first."

He bowed his head again. A little disappointment ebbed from him, and Ana wondered if she would need to keep the people disappointed rather than happy. She felt more at peace when she could taste their fear and hopelessness.

"You would follow as I directed?"

"You are my queen," he said, bowing again. "I would follow wherever you go, do anything as directed."

"Did you follow another?" she asked.

"Major Field was my commander." He bowed his head.

"You know who is loyal to me."

"The world is loyal, Majesty."

"You don't need to overdo it. I can read the mind of every man; I can taste the fear of the children. I can change your future in a blink."

The man gulped down a rising uncertainty, and Ana slowly licked her lips. "I could drink from you for days if I chose," she whispered, standing close. The man shivered, his fear increasing. "Or," she added carefully. He looked up, his confidence returning. "You demonstrate your loyalty and I make you stronger."

He nodded slowly.

"People would come to the regent," she said, taking a step back, and the soldier blinked as though woken from a spell. "They raised concerns, issues, petty grievances. Why do they not come to me as their queen?"

The man opened and closed his mouth several times, and she could taste the fear he considered in the people. "They do not need for anything," he said instead.

Ana allowed the darkness to fill her features, and the soldier stumbled back. "Do not lie to me," she growled.

"They fear what you will do," he said hurriedly.

"Assure them that I am open to listening. I am Queen and I want my world to thrive. That can only happen when the people are content." He stared at her for a moment longer before he nodded again. "Spread the word. I would like to hear the concerns of my kingdom. I will not harm anyone who comes with truth on their tongue."

He nodded again and hurried away. She reached out after him, and he stopped. Frozen mid-step. The fear increased in the man as she walked forward slowly. "I did not ask your name," she said, coming to stand in front of him.

"Grant," he murmured.

She stood to the side and waved him on. He stumbled forward on his way, headed to the barracks. As he disappeared inside, she wondered if he had been one of the men she had seen that day she'd hidden in the shadows of the bathhouse, when she had tried to determine what the world thought of her and whether they would support a king she no longer needed.

She would work on the people. She would find the boy and remove him when she needed to. The kingdom was hers and hers alone.

# 13

The last person the mage wanted to think of was the young king, but he couldn't shift him from his mind. Every step—every painful, dirty step—made him think of the boy and what hardship he must have endured to escape from the castle hoping for help. Only the mage wasn't confident he would be able to find help. Not out here, amongst the empty fields and rocky road, where the dust filled his mouth and nose and clothes.

Although, the king was young and determined. The mage was focused on escaping something very different. He didn't want to be caught by the queen's creatures. They were able to sneak up on him, and that worried him. In unfamiliar territory, in direct sunlight. He squinted up at the sky, trying to remember the last time he had willingly stood out in the sunshine or walked this distance in the sun.

And he couldn't. He must have run around at some stage as a young man, even as a boy, but it seemed he had lived in that workshop for so long he had no idea of the world outside it, nor even if he could find who he was looking for. Was he headed in the right direction?

He paused and looked over the green fields surrounding him. Each looked the same as the ones before, yet he had ridden this way with men not so long ago. Why was it so hard to remember?

The mage had been a man who led the people, had soldiers at

his beck and call, and now he was a man of the shadows. When had the change occurred, and was it due to the regent or Ana?

The mage did not want to admit that Ana scared him far more than when he had suggested to the regent that they leave her where she was. The moment he'd touched her, he had seen nothing but darkness. Hate, fear. But it had been linked to the king. How he had thought that he could make her something else with the king gone, something more than he had seen, he could no longer understand.

The mage paused and dusted at his clothing. He had ridden a horse, a magnificent beast who had been only too happy to carry him through the kingdom. He had searched the world for girls and magic he could use, or for an apprentice to create. The girls he had used to bring Ana to the capital had been such children. The twins he had tried to use to stop her had been similar, but he had travelled with others, moving at night or sending men to do as he wanted.

Now he was on his own, and it worried him far more than it should. He just had to find the king. He closed his eyes to the world and tried to stretch out his magic. Magic that he had used so often before to find something, anything, he could use. Nothing. He scratched at his hair and staggered on. His feet hurt, and he wondered why he hadn't taken a horse. He had been afforded whatever luxury he needed. Ana had not banished him or taken from him. Despite her own skill, she had not impeded on his.

He looked up again into the endless blue sky. The heat was getting to him. He had rushed away, certain he would have a chance to fix what had been done. He would win over the young king and in saving the kingdom, save himself.

He sighed at the sight of a small stand of trees ahead of him and hurried along the road hoping for some shade. He had at least taken a water skin, which he had been able to fill at the tavern. Even though it had been abandoned, he had found a well containing water and helped himself to some old cheese. It took him far longer than he would have liked to reach the cool shade of the trees, and he was thankful for the water. He was starting to feel like an old man, which surprised him.

The king must have come the same way. He could have passed the man when he returned to the capital after meeting Ana, and he wondered that it was the first time he had thought about it. Firstly, it would have been harder for the king to travel than he had expected, although he had made it further than the mage had ever thought possible. And they had been so close without him sensing the man at all. Although, he hadn't been looking for him; they hadn't realised he had gone, and the mage's mind had been on other things. That the young girl he'd thought would be his strongest ally would be his greatest enemy.

He laughed to himself, the sound strange after so long in silence. It echoed off the trees, and he froze, sure one of the shadows had moved. He studied the ground until his focus blurred, and the shadow only moved ever so slightly in line with the sun.

He didn't even know where the king was, he thought as he sat against a tree and closed his eyes. No one did, not even Ana. But then, she could send her shadows out into the world. He wondered if she might have a better idea of where he was even if she could not reach him.

He shook his head, trying to remove the idea of Ana. He seemed to know where she might be, even when she moved around. There were moments when he thought her gone, but then he could sense her just as strongly, usually around the castle.

He breathed out slowly, trying to empty his mind completely, allow a solution to come to him regarding the predicament he was in. And he hoped not in the shape of a shadow.

Through the darkness, a light glowed softly in the distance. He walked towards it, thinking it was a candle. But the strange soft light didn't flicker. Then Sarah came into view, and he wondered at the girl he had lost to the darkness. He was reminded of another. But as the girl before him started to disappear, he refocused on her and held out a hand for her to take. She didn't move, just stood glowing in the darkness.

"Can you hear me, child?" he asked.

She looked up but did not speak. She glowed a little brighter, and the shadows receded. Then the girl changed before his eyes. She grew into a young woman, one he recognised. Her blonde hair curled and her eyes glowed blue.

"I know you," he whispered.

As the woman looked at him, fear crossed her face. She glowed a little brighter again, and then she was gone.

The mage blinked into the light, waking from the dream and looking around the trees. Night was coming. The hot sun had sunk low on the horizon, lighting the world in an orange glow. Had he imagined what he had seen? For the king's friend was like Sarah. There was a glow, a magic he couldn't quite grasp. He closed his eyes again and tried to remember what he had seen. She had not spoken to him, but there was a green light behind her, as though the sunshine filtered through foliage.

They must be in the forest. He stretched out his senses but still found nothing. He wondered if he had lost his magic and Ana was in control. He had an understanding of where her strength and magic came from, but she was far more than that. She was stronger than she should be. She'd had a magic before, an innate skill, a strength. And yet now she was more. He was reminded of her mother and the strength within. She had not been able to live with it and had willingly given it away in the end, although that had done nothing to help her or him.

He sighed, resting his head back and looking out between the trees at the changing world around him. He would continue to the forest in the hope of finding the king there.

The breeze blew through the leaves, rustling the world around him, but the shadows were just that. No matter how hard he looked, he could not see them. But they had always been able to hide from him. Even the maid, who had visited so often and helped him in some ways, would never be what she had been.

"I don't think this is a good idea," Ed whispered as they made their way back through the dark grass fields towards the lord's castle.

"He does," Belle said.

"It was only recently that Ana sent her creatures and then appeared herself," Forest said.

Ed wished he could see Dray in the dark to get an idea of what he thought. He had been keen enough to leave before, and now he was following along with Belle. He stopped amongst the stalks, hoping they were headed in the right direction, and Belle pulled at his hand.

He had the niggling feeling of uncertainty, not about where they were going but whom he was with. They talked more than they had, Dray showing an interest where he had not previously. He had been focused only on Ana not so long ago, to the distraction of everything else. Now it was Belle.

"What do you see in her?" Ed blurted, and Belle shushed him.

"Who are you talking to?" Forest asked quietly behind him.

Ed opened his mouth and then closed it. Now was not the time, not in the dark when they had no idea how close the creatures were. And he did not want the lord to think of him as a jealous king. Not that he was King, despite what some still called him. He was just a boy again, with a girl, looking for a way to find his crown. He sighed, and Belle squeezed his hand before tugging him faster through the crops. The night was Ana's time, when she was at her strongest, or so he would have thought. He remembered her stepping out of the darkness in the stairwell where he had been talking with Dray about the state of the world and whether or not they could trust her.

"She no longer seems to know where we are," Dray whispered

through the stalks ahead of him. "Or she no longer cares."

"It is like you have her skill of reading minds," Ed said unkindly.

"We can have this discussion when we reach the castle."

Ed bit back a further sigh and nodded, not that the man could see him in the dark. But he no longer knew with Dray just what skill the man did have. What if she had replaced him with a shadow creature long ago? What if, like Kemp, he was something else? Before Ed could express his concerns, they reached the edge of the field.

Torches lit up the world around the castle, but Ed was sure they wouldn't be enough to stop Ana if that was their intent. It might have been to just keep the shadows at bay. He wondered what others were doing around the kingdom to protect themselves from their new queen.

They moved forward when the lord appeared in a doorway, Dray in the lead and Belle dragging Ed with her not far behind.

"Thank you," the lord said as they entered the building. The small entrance hall was a surprise, more in the lack of men with the lord than the size of the space.

"We trust that this is the right thing to do," Belle said softly.

"I'm not sure I agree," Ed said before thinking, and the whole group turned on him. "I expressed this before. Forgive me," he said to the lord, bowing his head. "She could be watching. She could have left others to watch in her stead."

Belle opened her mouth to protest, and he shook his head. "Once she knows we are here, we are not the only ones in danger."

"If she is looking," Dray repeated.

"What does she want?" Ed asked the group.

"She appears to want to rule as others have before her, to do what she can for the kingdom." It was the lord who answered him, indicating a doorway from the hallway. "She is focused on other things."

"What is the main threat to the one with the crown?" Ed asked.

"She has no threats. She could destroy anyone and everyone if that was her wish."

"But is it? If she wants to rule, to be a queen, then—like any before her, such as my uncle—she would be worried about the people wanting someone else. Like a king born from a favourite king. Someone who has a right to it. Not someone who stole it."

"I heard you gave it away," a snide voice offered from the shadows. Despite his best efforts, Ed flinched. The boy stepped from the shadows, and he recognised the lord's son.

"And what would you like from our queen?" Ed asked.

"That is not why we have asked you here," the lord said firmly.

Ed looked between father and son, then turned his attention back to Belle.

"They know you are the king," she said without hesitation, "and they will support you."

He sighed, wanting to believe them, but nowhere was safe from her anymore. Nowhere was as it had been.

"You toured the provinces," the lord said, catching him by surprise, and he shook his head. "You wanted to be king."

"I ran away," Ed said. Although the lord maintained his stoic features, the son openly gaped. "I went to find help, advice, some meaning," he said, clutching for the same again now. "I found friends to help me regain what was mine," he added as his breathing returned to normal. Although one of those friends had not only tried to end him, but had stolen what she'd been helping him regain.

"You were in the forest. I heard that you had visited the mountains."

Ed nodded slowly. "I made the claim to my uncle that I was travelling. I didn't want the people to know I had run; I didn't know what my responsibility was."

The lord nodded slowly. "You were not given an opportunity. And then when you were, your trust was in the wrong people. I understand why you are reluctant now to accept my help, but I can assure you, Your Majesty, that I am willing to help. I would like to see you on the throne."

"You may very well have signed your own death sentence with those words," Forest muttered, looking around the room. Ed focused on Dray, who was looking into the corner. Ed followed his gaze and found he stared at nothing. Dray had once had the ability to know where Ana was, but this too appeared to have been severed with the loss of her link to them.

"What can you see?" Ed eventually asked, unable to wait any longer.

"Nothing," Dray murmured, his eyes still fixed on the wall. In the following silence, he turned around and looked at Ed. "I am not what you want me to be."

"You have always been far more than I could need from you, and yet I am still unsure whether I know you or not. Or know what you can do, or what you want to be able to do."

"Ed," Belle said, a warning in her tone.

"He worries about the relationship I had with Ana and now what I am to you, or you to me."

Belle blinked at Ed, then raised her eyebrows in question. She knew exactly what she was to him, despite his poor word choice. She knew that he loved no one but her. And as much as he wanted to believe she felt the same, believe the words she told him repeatedly, there was a doubt where the large soldier was involved.

"Don't let her come between us. She didn't when she was the girl from Sheer Rock, or even when she was a witch trying to help you. She is not that girl."

Ed nodded once, hearing the sadness and loss in the large man's voice and feeling her loss almost as much as he did. Dray was right; Ana was gone, and he shouldn't allow what memory there was of her to come between them. They were all they had left; this was his family.

"She will come when you need her to," Dray murmured, looking more at Forest.

"The queen?" the lord asked.

"Salima," Ed said. "Another friend." And he hoped a way to find an answer to this.

"We cannot fight," Belle whispered.

"We're not," Ed said, looking to Dray, who perhaps gave him a small smile with only one corner of his mouth turned up slightly. He looked too serious all the time, and Ed was reminded of his laughing with Belle not long ago. "But I think we should be headed for the forest. There are those who could help us there."

"I have heard the forest people have disappeared," the lord said, regaining Ed's attention.

"Disappeared?"

"Perhaps they are hiding," Forest offered. Belle nodded slowly.

"I am not sure what you think we can do for you," Ed said to the lord.

"I asked you here so that I could help you. I wasn't sure that I could, but when the queen appeared in my hall, I knew there was no option but to help you. Despite the fact that you had gone."

"Gone?" Ed asked.

"I have heard the stories. I know what she can see, what she understands even when you don't want her to. I thought you were gone, on your way far from here, and I had not offered you any help because I didn't think I had anything to offer, or that I should. She appeared to believe me."

Ed looked the older man over. "Are you sure?"

"I believed the words I told her; the boy knew no different. And so we were safe to reassure her and then come back to you."

"That was some risk," Ed said.

"And one you might have lost. She could be watching," Forest grumbled.

"Why would she? The queen wants my loyalty. She wants me to give to her as I gave to others before her. She wants to be Queen, and she wants all that goes with that, not just the power, not just the fear."

"Although I think she takes some delight in that." Dray's deep voice was quiet and sad.

"I met your father. We were friends of a sort. His father worked with mine. Your uncle, no matter how different, was in many ways the same. It is the way the world works. She might have wanted something different when she started—she might have had an idea of something different—but in the end they all want the same, and it is my place as Lord of this province to provide."

For the first time in longer than he could remember, Ed felt a weight lift from his shoulders. There was a little bit of hope that maybe, when all was said and done, Ana was just like anyone else who had wanted power, usurped a throne, stolen a crown. And that she was someone it could all be taken back from.

Only this queen had power they didn't fully understand and an army of shadow creatures who could each destroy the world, with no way to stop them.

# 14

Barlow enjoyed the freedom the forest allowed. His mental exhaustion had slowly started to lift, yet it felt as though time moved differently beneath the trees. Despite the number of days they had camped beneath the canopy, the forest people and their lord said little to them. The people had allowed them to stay, but they weren't invited to be part of the group. There was a lack of trust, and the lord had been burned by his sister. There were moments when someone would raise her name or hint about her, and he would not react as a grieving brother should.

On the edge of the camp was the other man—shirtless, leather pants, long dark hair, unusual ears. Always watching from the edge of the clearing. But whenever Barlow made a move to get closer to the man or talk to him, he disappeared into the trees. Barlow had become far more frustrated with the situation than he had expected.

"Have you seen the king?" Barlow asked the lord, who was standing by the fire.

His focus was on the flames, but his mind was clearly elsewhere as he slowly shook his head.

"What can you tell me of the man in the trees?" Barlow asked.

The lord looked up then and into the trees, as though someone might be watching them, but the other man was gone.

"He led us here," Barlow prompted.

"They are watching over us, helping us by allowing us to stay in the forest. We haven't done as we should for the trees, and this is as much as they will do. I think they watch to ensure we don't endanger the forest any further."

"Endanger the forest?" Barlow asked.

The lord turned back to the flames. "All I can do now is keep my people safe."

"Would you fight for the king?"

The man didn't move, didn't even indicate that he had heard the question.

"I know she seems…"

"She is far more than we could ever imagine, let alone defeat. Have you seen what they can do?" The lord looked up then, his eyes wide with fear.

Barlow nodded once. He had seen far more than even this man in the time since the queen had settled on the throne. And if he were to return to her without the king, he was sure to see far worse. No matter what title she gave him or promises she made. There would be someone else who would step into his place. Someone willing to do whatever it took to make her happy, to get the title or the power, or whatever it was she offered. Despite their feelings for the king, Barlow knew there were too many amongst the King's Men who would gladly follow her.

Standing by the silent lord, he looked into the flames, the same fear overwhelming him of what they could do to defeat this woman. She might have scared the people, forced many into hiding, but there would be those like the soldiers who were willing to listen. And if she promised them stability, they would be willing to follow her.

Barlow thought of the young king trying to convince the people he should be given the chance to take over what his father had intended. They had listened, but he had seen many faces in the crowd, heard whispers in the market that they were well enough under the regent—why change the way of the world? The king had then given the crown to the witch.

Some would feel it changed nothing; others could not forgive him. Barlow sighed, feeling that they were lost no matter what he did. Even if he gathered support for the king, found the young man and helped him make it back to the castle.

"I don't know how to fix this," he murmured.

"I don't know that we can," the lord returned. For the first time in all the days he had watched him, Barlow thought about how the surly, stubborn man had changed. He was quiet, focused on the people and not what any of this meant for him.

"All the times you demanded payment." Barlow watched the man beside him, seeing the lord of a province for the first time, not a young man who thought he was more than he was.

"I didn't understand what was truly important," he said, his gaze still on the flames. "Dahli could have been something great," he added softly.

"She was," Barlow said, but he wondered if the queen had stolen her or if she had asked for something more.

"She wasn't in the end. She was something very different. We might all become such creatures if she wants that, for we have no way to stop it."

Barlow considered the lord's words. He knew full well just what the queen was capable of. There was always a way for her to win. "She can't penetrate the forest," he whispered. "She can't send her children after us."

"Not yet," the lord said. "Can we hide here forever? Will she find a way to reach us?"

"The Near Folk don't leave the forest," Barlow said.

"We are joined to the trees. We can leave. We choose not to," said the man who had watched them for so long. Barlow looked up at him standing on the other side of the fire.

"She was here once," Barlow said.

The man nodded once. "We felt the magic within, shared our magic with her, but she was different then."

"Would she know your magic?"

The man stared at him across the flames, and the lord looked up as well.

"You can't answer," Barlow eventually said for him. "The king was worried that the girl he knew had been replaced by one of the creatures she directs."

"It is not so, and yet it is," the man said. "If the king comes, we will help him if we can."

"*If* he comes? He hasn't yet? I thought this would be the best place for him."

"It might be, and yet he is not here. It may be hard for him to reach us."

Barlow looked behind him to the three men sitting by their makeshift camp, on the edge of all that was occurring around them. As soon as they left the trees, they would be lost; the creatures would be with them, would follow them or destroy them. He wanted to do all he could to protect the king, but in that moment, he couldn't face the idea of leaving the safety of the trees.

"The time will come," the Near man said, and when Barlow turned back, he was gone.

Belle stood at the window and looked out over the sea of green stalks. The soft movement was calming as the stalks swayed in the wind. She searched them for signs of something or someone moving through the fields. From the ground she would be able to see if someone had entered a field, even someone with skill, and yet the only visible tracks through the fields were the pathways already marked. They had entered the castle from the other direction the night before, and she was sure, thinking of Ed, that if she were to look over those fields, she would very clearly see the bent stalks.

"Why are you so sure this is a good idea?" Ed asked. She tried not to flinch at the sound of his voice, having been unaware that anyone else was in the room.

"I just know we need all the help we can gather."

"The son might be a bigger risk than the lord himself. He would not keep any secrets for us, even if he were able to. She was here, Belle—she was in this very building, searching the minds of those within it."

"And she thought us gone," Belle said, turning slowly to him. "She would not expect us to return; she would not suspect him of helping us."

"You can't be sure," Ed stammered. She could see the fear and anger rising within him. He wanted to believe her, and yet he had seen too much. "We can't be sure of anything."

She crossed the room and reached for his hands. "You trust me," she said, and he nodded slowly although she didn't need him to. "I trust that you can gather the forces required to find a way to end Ana's rule and regain your crown. This man is a way to do that."

Ed sighed and leaned forward to rest his forehead on hers. "Ending this," he said softly, "might mean killing her. Will Dray do that?"

"He will do whatever is needed to save his king. Don't doubt him."

Ed sighed. As he made to move away, Belle squeezed his hands and refused to let him go.

"Don't doubt me," she whispered.

He pressed his lips to hers then, dropping her hands to wrap his arms around her and pull her close to his chest.

As he released his hold, she smiled up at him. "I know you doubt me."

"It is not doubt," he said, taking a step back from her. "It is fear."

She looked after him, waiting for him to explain himself. "Ed," she prompted when he didn't continue.

"He is a good man, a stronger man than I am. He listens to you when I question. I am not like him."

She laughed, and he scowled. "I love you," she said. "And he is a good man, but he still loves another, and he follows you. He would do anything you asked of him."

Ed nodded, and she wondered if he would ask Dray to leave them. "It is time to meet with the lord. Will you come with me?" he asked.

She nodded and took the hand he held out to her, and they walked together towards the lord's room. She had thought they would meet more formally, but the small room they entered was only the size of the cottage they had lived in. It had a large bed at one end and several chairs around a cosy fire. As they entered, the lord stood and indicated a chair for Ed, then the one he had just vacated for Belle. She smiled but took a chair further from the flames to allow them to sit closer together.

"I don't think we need advertise to many that you are here," he said.

"Your son knows," Ed said quickly, "and servants."

"Only those I can trust. And I hope that you will be long gone if the woman returns, and my son will not have an understanding as to why you were really here."

"He might guess."

"He is not what I hoped he would be."

"But will he help us or work against us?" Ed pressed.

The older man sighed, and Belle wondered at what Ed hoped to gain by this. His focus was on the trees, but she knew there was more. They needed the support of the kingdom if they were to take her on, because it would not be easy no matter what they did.

"We need you." Belle did not want to interrupt Ed, but she had the feeling their time was limited.

"It is not as easy as you want it to be," the lord said, turning towards her.

"It is not going to be easy," she said. "I am well aware of that. She is strong, too strong for us. We need to find a way to be able to meet her, not just in strength but without giving her the chance to gather her forces."

"Will it be enough?"

"Perhaps not," Belle admitted. "They can move so fast, use the shadows…" She had wanted to gain his support. She knew he was important, although she couldn't articulate why that was. But the more she tried to convince him, the harder it seemed. "I should leave you two to talk," she said, standing.

"You have a gift," the lord said quickly, standing to meet her. "You know more than you should."

She nodded, although she was far from understanding just what she was.

"You have seen me in this," he said, but it wasn't a question.

"Do you understand what I am?"

He smiled as he indicated the chair, and she sat back down slowly. "My wife had a gift. It wasn't clear just what that was, and she didn't want to explore it any further. The mage visited with us, pleaded for her to learn from him, but she said it would end badly."

"She saw that," Belle whispered.

"She never told me what she saw, but if she told me not to go somewhere, not to meet with someone or to do something, I never questioned her." He looked towards the fire. "When she told me we were expecting our second child, she cried."

"She knew she would die," Belle whispered.

He nodded.

"I am sorry," Ed said with a glance around at Belle. She knew he wondered what she might see. But she shook her head. She felt things, but she had no real certainty of the future. Not like the lord's wife might have. But when they had arrived and met him, she had known, felt that they had to convince him to help, that he would help. Perhaps she would have to wait for something else to tell her if she would be lost or not. Ed's focus was all on her.

"I want to help, but gathering forces to fight her would let her know what we plan."

"Can we consider something else—part of a plan, a meeting point—without considering the outcome?"

"Once we are in the open, we are not safe," the lord said.

"No," Ed murmured. "We have the same fear. A meeting of lords. Could you send word to the others to meet somewhere central, to discuss tribute or how best to serve your queen."

"We haven't done such a thing since your father's time," he said. "And that was at the capital."

Ed looked back to Belle, and she shook her head slowly. She wasn't sure where they needed to be, but not the capital—not Ana's territory. They had to lure her away to somewhere they were stronger. She sighed, closing her eyes.

"You were headed to the forest," the lord prompted. "Why?"

"The trees," Belle murmured. Then she looked up at the man. "The forest could be a safe place."

"It is also far from most of the kingdom and the capital. There are several of us who would have to pass through the capital to reach it, or travel far more slowly through the kingdom if we don't take the main roads. We will be very visible, and she will want to know what we are doing."

"You could invite her."

"When we are not taking the meeting to her?" the lord asked.

"I don't know," Belle murmured, closing her eyes.

"You were gone for some time," Dray said as they entered the rooms they had been given. "Did you determine a plan?"

Ed sighed, and Belle walked directly to the window. Dray was tempted to join her, for she would have a better idea of where they were going next, but the watchful eyes of the king made him stop. He knew the man trusted him, yet he was uncertain of something.

"We talked in circles, trying to find a way to outsmart a woman we have no way to outguess. It would take nothing for her to appear amongst us, or any group travelling across the kingdom." Ed rubbed at his eyes. "What do we do?" he asked the woman at the window who didn't appear to be listening.

"The trees," she whispered against the glass. "The only way is to the trees."

"Then that is what we do," Dray said, stepping forward. "The rest can work out where they stand. If the most important thing is to get the king to the Near Folk, let us focus on that. The queen will work out what we are doing sooner or later, and it might be worth the distraction from the lord and what he might do to assist."

Belle turned slowly from the window and looked at him as though trying to read him. She nodded once.

"Near Forest it is," Ed said, drawing Dray's attention, but he seemed comfortable with the idea. "We had planned for this before we were called back here. The man was always going to support us, but it is of comfort to know it. When?" he asked Belle.

She shrugged and turned back to the window.

Ed then looked to Dray and indicated the woman with his head. Dray studied the man, unsure if he was seeing what he was. Then Ed walked to the table and sat silently beside Forest. "Salima will find us when she needs to," he reassured the sword master. Dray stepped up beside Belle and looked over his shoulder at the king, who was now talking in hushed tones with the other man.

Belle stood at the window, her eyes closed to the view. Dray reached out slowly and placed a hand on her shoulder. "You don't need to know it all," he said.

"I already know far more than I would wish," she said, turning back to him. She looked at him with sad eyes as he lifted his hand slowly from her shoulder. "I know," she repeated.

"I don't need to," Dray said with a smile. He was what he was, and he had never really expected to live long. Not to become an old man, at any rate. He was a soldier, and his career was already over. "As long as we can stop her," he said.

"I don't know that, but we can try."

There was a sharp rap at the door. Before any of them could consider what to do, it opened and revealed the lord's son.

"I would like to help," he said too loudly, his grin too wide, and Dray was reminded of the shadow creatures. As though reading the thought, he then turned to Ed and bowed smoothly.

Dray let out the breath he had been holding, but his hand rested on his sword.

"Help with what?" Ed asked.

"Whatever it is my father has promised," the boy continued.

"He has promised me nothing," Ed said, his face clear of emotion.

Belle had edged behind Dray, her hand touching lightly over his fingers against his sword. "We go now," she whispered, so faint he wasn't sure he'd heard her, and then the boy turned his focus on them.

"I am on your side," he said, his eyes on Dray's sword.

"Your father is loyal to the queen," Dray answered. "I'm not sure why we are here; he will not support us."

"He met with you," the boy stammered, his confidence slipping.

"Courtesy to my father. But he does not see me as King. It seems no one does anymore, and we will be leaving the province as soon as we can."

"I don't believe you," the boy said, but his voice betrayed him.

"I don't care what you believe. Your father has housed us here long enough, possibly while he alerts others to our presence. We will leave."

The young man stepped to the side as though waiting for them to exit the room. And then he closed the still-open door. "I will accompany you."

"To where? And at a risk to your father? He might not support me, but he is still a lord of Ilia. I would not like to see him risked."

"Risked?" the young man asked.

"If the queen learns you travel with us, who do you think she will punish?"

The boy moved uncertainly from foot to foot, looking over the group as though trying to determine where he fit, what they really wanted and what it might mean for his father.

"When we are free," Ed said, stepping forward, "I will remember this."

The boy grinned again and nodded. "There are fine horses in the stable."

Ed looked to the sword master and then back to the boy.

"If they were stolen, my father would be very upset."

Ed nodded once, and the boy bowed and left the room. Dray watched after him for too long. He doubted the boy would allow them to ride off without some effort to join them. But the risk if he followed was far greater to them all, not just the lord. Ed was right—if they weren't careful of who they collected along the way, it might do more harm than good. But then the more they had to reach the trees, the better the chances.

Dray turned to the woman still standing behind him. She breathed out softly, as though she had been holding her breath. "Is it the boy, or is it something else?" he asked her.

"I don't want him to come, but I fear he will follow. And I'm not sure what that will mean."

"I will follow your instructions."

The king coughed politely behind him, but he didn't turn around. This woman was to be listened to. He understood that there was more to her than even she understood, but if they were going to survive this, she would be the reason they survived.

# 15

Ana stood in the middle of the throne room and breathed in the cool stone that surrounded her. The window had been painted over, dulling the light within the room. The child appeared before her, bowed low and then grinned a wide toothy smile. It made Ana shiver with anticipation.

"We have found them," the child hissed.

"Where I expected?"

"Yes, Majesty." The long tongue flicked out across the scaly skin. "They prepare to leave."

"Is the boy to travel with them?"

"They have tried to put him off, but he will follow. She understands that."

"Did you locate the mage?" Ana asked, walking slowly around the creature standing upright in the room.

"He walks towards the forest. He is further from the capital than I thought him capable, but he is far from the trees. Too far from the trees."

"Perfect," she hummed, running her hand over the creature's arm as she made her way back to her throne. "How strong is she?"

"She barely glows."

Ana held tight to the armrest. What she planned had risk, but she needed to separate them. She might not be able to reach them quite as easily as she could have, but at least she knew where they were.

"Take several of the others with you. Not that I fear for you, rather I would like you to create a little more fear. You know what to do?"

The creature bowed down low before her.

"The lord's boy," she said as the creature started to disappear into the shadows of the room. "Bring him to me if he follows them. I am curious as to what he could be."

"Majesty," the creature hissed, then disappeared.

Ana sighed with the relief of the empty room. The calm and quiet. The sound of soldiers' armour squeaking outside the door disturbed her thoughts. But as the man took his place by the door, she realised his armour was not as shiny as it had been. It was also smooth, the usual emblem not pressed into the metal. She wondered why she had not thought of changing it, putting her own stamp on the world of Ilia, although in many ways she had. The soldier bowed his head and remained at attention.

She wanted desperately to see what the others were doing, but she settled again, and the sound of people filled her ears. She tried not to grumble aloud as several men were ushered into the room. They seemed more than reluctant. Her new favourite soldier was just behind.

"Majesty," he said with a smile. "Please allow me to present the people. They have much to discuss with you."

She stood slowly as more people flowed into the room, and the older man at the front of the line shivered in obvious fear.

"I heard these men very clearly articulating their issues at an inn. They had travelled from the grasslands."

"I was only in the grasslands recently myself," Ana said sweetly, waving the man forward. "I found your lord quite obliging. What issue do you have that he cannot assist you with?"

"The level of tribute I pay, Your…" He stammered as Ana glared at him. "Majesty," he added weakly.

"Tribute is how we survive. It is how we show our loyalty to those who help us, protect us and rule over us."

He bowed his head. "I have not enough to feed my family," he said.

"Yet you can travel all this way. Did you leave your family behind?"

"I thought if I could find work in the capital…" He lifted his head, unsure how to continue. Ana could see the man's family in his mind, but there was little guilt at leaving them. More relief.

"Who will feed your family now that you are here?" she asked.

"My brother will watch over them. He has had a better crop, and he can afford to give and feed them all." A wave of jealousy from the man strengthened Ana.

"I could give you a job," she said, sitting slowly in the throne and leaning back. Her movements were slow, but the fear in the room increased.

The man nodded once.

"You understand what that would be?"

He nodded again.

"Wait there," she said, indicating a place by the opposite wall.

He stood and, without another word, moved across the room.

The next man was nudged forward. "I only wish to go home," he stammered.

Ana closed her eyes, looking into the hot sun of the man's mind. He longed for family, for familiar ground. "What do you do?" she asked.

"I am a miner," he said, bowing suddenly. He had forgotten to do so before, but she didn't mind. He would strengthen the kingdom; he provided wealth that could be shared. She saw it move from hand to hand.

"Why have you come?"

He looked up at the soldier beside him and then back to her. "The lands between here and my home are not safe. There are many stories, and I feared…"

"I will return you home," she whispered. She called forth one of her children, one of the many new ones. Ana closed her eyes and reached for the child. When her hand found its, she thought of the man's family. "Take him home and ensure he is safe," she whispered.

The man backed up as the child moved effortlessly towards him, the fluid movement something she had not seen in her children.

"When you have delivered him, return to my side," she said.

The child bowed its head. "Majesty." Then it took the man by the arm and they were both gone.

The next man in the line was backing up, and the soldier nudged him forward. The room was becoming unbearable as panic moved through the people. They murmured, cursing and insisting they be released. Ana was drinking in the mayhem when the child reappeared. Silence once again filled the room, although the same level of fear remained.

"He is safe," the child hissed. "Although the children were frightened."

"They will come to trust," Ana said. "I wish for you to wait beside me."

"Majesty." It smoothly bowed its head and stepped behind the throne.

The man who had been trying to retreat then stepped forward on his own, bowed low before her and dropped to a knee. "Majesty," he said.

They were not far from the castle when Belle pulled her horse to a stop in the middle of the road. They had been given free passage, the lord making a show of not trusting them and sending them away. The disappointed son hung back in the room, and although Belle had not seen him, she knew he wasn't far behind. But that was not the reason she had stopped. Uncertainty filled her.

She had been so sure they needed to leave the castle, and yet something else she had not understood was coming.

"Belle?" Dray asked.

She shook her head as she turned back to the group, but her eyes sought out Ed. She had the sudden feeling she would not see him again. As the feeling started to overwhelm her, the shadow appeared in the middle of the group and the horses pranced about.

Fear and anger flared in her chest, and the creature squinted at her. "You still don't scare me," it hissed.

"Kemp?" Dray asked as another creature appeared from the shadows of the crop.

The creature only had eyes for her. Dray drew his sword, as did Ed and Forest, but two more creatures emerged from the shadows.

Belle could feel the uncertainty. Although the creatures could kill them all within a heartbeat, no one moved other than the horses, and as the creature in the centre of the group held up a hand, they stopped.

"I will not die here," she murmured. One of the creatures behind her groaned. As she turned on it, it disappeared. She focused on Kemp in the middle of the group. His grin widened, and his long tongue licked the air around it. Belle shivered.

The creature that had disappeared reappeared on the other side of the group. Too close to Ed. As he flinched, Belle was distracted, and then the darkness closed in around her as Ed screamed.

Belle sucked in a deep breath as the shadow passed and the sunshine warmed her skin. She had travelled through the shadows before, and she wondered how far she had come. But she wasn't back at the castle. She was on a road, dusty but wide, and fields stretched out on either side as far as she could see. She turned slowly, taking in the forest in the distance. She had been this way before. As she turned again, sure that the capital was not far away, the mage was standing in the middle of the road.

She stepped back slowly, and his surprised expression changed as a grin very similar to the creature's spread across his face.

"Well this is a turn of events," he said. "How nice to meet you."

"It is not nice to meet you," Belle murmured. "Why are we here?" She looked around then and realised just how alone they were, how far from the capital. "Where is your horse, carriage, soldiers?"

"I headed out on my own," he said, giving a little shrug with one shoulder.

"Alone?" Belle asked, wondering just what Ana wanted by putting her in this situation.

"I was looking for the boy," he said, somewhat defensively.

"You didn't know she was going to put me here?" Belle said.

"Who knows what that woman will do?" he grunted. "She had wanted me to do something, which I refused, and then I thought if I could find the boy…" He sighed and ran his fingers through his rough cropped hair, which stood straight up.

Belle laughed. There was nothing else she could do. She was far from everyone she wanted to be with, with a man who thought he had found a way around the queen. "No one can," she murmured aloud.

"No one can what?" he asked.

"Outsmart the witch," Belle said. "You have done just as she needed you to. We thought we could hide our intentions and our location, and yet she found us easily."

"You were with the boy? Did she take him?" His voice was a little more hurried than she expected.

Belle shook her head. She had no idea what might have happened to the others. "All I know is that there were many of them and I am here."

"The forest?"

"Pardon?"

"Were you in the forest, girl?" he snapped, any kindness gone.

Belle crossed her arms and glared at the old man. He stared back in return, then sighed and looked along the road to the north.

"I was going to the forest," he said, his voice soft.

"As were we," Belle admitted.

"Then we shall continue that way. It might be that we can find the boy together and a way around this mess."

"She knows where you are," Belle said. "She will know where we both are."

"It doesn't matter. She doesn't think me a threat. That is why she has put you with me. She thinks I will use you, that you will fight me to get back to the boy."

"He isn't a boy," Belle interrupted. "And why won't I fight you?"

"Because I know what you are. And I can help you discover that. Together we might be able to stop her."

Belle laughed again, a mad cackle. There was no stopping Ana. Whatever she was, wherever her magic had come from, she controlled the world. No matter what Belle thought she might be able to do, Ana would still win. She had been playing with them. They didn't have a chance, and Ana had known that all along.

"You saw the girl glow," the mage said, dragging her from her thoughts.

Belle nodded once.

"You can do that," he said. When she shook her head, he smiled again, only it was soft and friendly. For a moment she was reminded of her father. "I can teach you how to control that."

Belle blinked slowly as the man continued to smile, and then she nodded slowly. He indicated along the road and, as he walked, she fell into step beside him.

They walked in silence. The mage glanced at her from time to time, but he was slow, and there were times she hoped he could travel faster.

"How many days have you been walking?"

"Couldn't honestly tell you."

"And you haven't seen shadow creatures."

"Although they appeared to have seen me. They hide too well."

"And they could still be watching every move we make," Belle said.

The older man beside her stopped, and she continued for a little while before she too stopped and turned back to take him in. She had only seen this man briefly in the capital, and yet in many ways she thought she knew him from the stories Ana and Ed had told her.

"You have hope," he said eventually, but he made no move to continue.

She waited. She did have hope, just a little bit, and with every step it was becoming smaller and smaller.

"We have no way to win against this woman," the mage said, taking a shaky step forward.

"And yet we both continue. I don't know if it is hope or something else. But I can't abandon Ed. I can't believe that this is what life will be."

"It is what life is," he said, his smile sad. "We have all sacrificed for the life we wanted. And yet we don't have it, nor will we, no matter the sacrifice."

"She was willing to put us together. Whether that was to hurt Ed or me, I don't know. And she may not believe we can make it to the trees, but I know we can be together again."

He nodded once, but she wasn't sure what he might be agreeing to, and he started his slow walk again.

# 16

Salima stretched her arms above her head and looked out across the sand. It would not be long now. The witch was playing with them, and it wasn't that she was confident in the game she played—she was in control. But something had changed, and although Salima wasn't sure exactly what that was, it did mean things were moving faster than she expected.

"Would you have destroyed her in the mountains?" she asked Ende, who sat on his usual rock looking in the same direction. He saw much, but not as she did, and she wondered at the differences between them.

"No," he sighed. "Despite what I saw, I couldn't."

"You saw the darkness," Salima whispered.

"What do you think we can do? Burn it away? Would you eat her?"

Salima turned to find him grinning and smiled with him. The idea of swallowing the woman in a single bite was odd and yet tempting. She wondered for a moment if the witch would be as warm and comforting inside her as she had been when Salima was a lost child searching for a brother she didn't know she had. But then she thought of the darkness within Ana and what that would do inside her.

"How do we shine a light on that darkness?" she asked. "Could it be as simple as burning it away?"

"I thought you saw it all," Ende replied, but there wasn't malice in his voice; there was surprise.

"I don't know what it is. I can see darkness. I can see Ed needing us to remove it from the world. But is it that easy, or will it be that hard?"

He smiled sadly at her and shook his head. They would all lose so much more than they already had. Of that she was certain.

❊

"You can't give up," Dray said.

Ed sat in the middle of the road, his head in his hands. Dray glanced at Forest, who just shook his head. They had been in the same place now for hours, and he was running out of nice ways to coax the king onward.

"She will find us wherever we are. She is just playing with us," Ed moaned.

"If she knew where we were earlier, she would have done something. We should not have returned to the Lord of the Grassland," Dray murmured.

"But we did, and now Belle is lost and Ana knows exactly where we are headed."

"And if she wanted to stop us doing that, she would have. If she wanted us dead, we would be. If she wanted us as part of her dark shadow army, we would be." Dray spoke firmly, his hand on his sword, with a familiar longing for his armour. "I will always be a member of the King's Men," he told himself.

"They are no longer the King's Men," Ed said, but something had shifted in the way he hunched over himself. He sighed as he held out a hand, and Dray pulled him to his feet. "Do you think there are any of them left beneath the armour?"

"I hope so," Dray said, feeling the relief at the king's change in attitude. "We have a long way to go." He rested his hand on Ed's shoulder. "We, you, have much to do."

Ed nodded slowly. "Thank you," he said. "Both of you," he added, looking at the sword master.

"We haven't done very much." The man looked towards the north, then lifted the bag at his feet up and over his shoulder and nodded to the king.

"She is playing with us," Ed said, a slight waver in his voice.

"But maybe we can win. We have the kingdom behind you. She can't rule with fear alone."

"She might win them over," Ed murmured.

Dray gave him a not quite respectful slap on the back, which got him moving along the road a few paces. Dray adjusted the strap of the pack the king carried and then nudged him again. "Then we win them back," Dray said. "But we can't do that here."

Ed finally nodded and climbed up on the horse who stood patiently waiting, chewing away at fresh green stalks at the side of the road. Dray waited a moment to ensure the king was going to stay on his mount, and then he too mounted his horse, as did the sword master. They faced north, and the king urged his horse forward slowly.

Dray didn't know how long it would be before she would send the shadows after them again. He kicked his horse into a faster gait, and the others followed along the road that led north. He didn't know how long they could follow this road either, but it was clear that the creatures knew just where they were and could use anyone to reach them at any time. Her link to them might have been broken, but the kingdom was small when he considered the power she had.

As the sky began to darken, despite riding hard, they found they were still in a territory similar to where they had been. The only difference was that the crops were shorter and there appeared to be less farms around. Not that they had seen many people in the grassland, but many smaller tracks had led off the road they had followed between the tall grasses.

They made camp at the side of the road, not wanting to

disappear too far from it in case they couldn't find it again. "Phillip had said the farm was gone," Ed murmured, looking into the small fire Forest had put together.

"When?" Forest asked, surprising Dray. It was the first word he had spoken in a long time.

"When we were in the forest. I was headed north, and they were to head home. Life might have been different if they had returned south then."

"And you wouldn't have got to know Belle as well as you did," the older man said with a smirk, which surprisingly made Ed smile.

"But they didn't have to come, and he told Belle the farm was gone."

"The farm we stayed at?" Dray asked.

Ed nodded. "Why would he do that?"

"Perhaps he thought it gone. It doesn't matter now. We can't undo all that has been done. I sometimes wonder what the world would be if I had let her fall," Dray admitted. Despite what Ana was now, he missed her and was grateful that he'd had the chance to know her, if only for a little while.

"You aren't that kind of man," Ed said.

"You sound like Belle," Dray said with a laugh.

Something made a noise in the darkness that surrounded them. All three were on their feet in an instant, swords drawn.

"We can't kill them with swords," Forest muttered.

"No," Dray said. "But holding it makes me feel better."

They sat back down, each looking into the fire and then beyond. It was going to be a long night. It was going to be a hard journey, but then that was what they seemed to do.

A young man walked out of the darkness, and they were on their feet again. He bowed his head and stood silently just in the firelight. They looked between each other and then back to the young man.

"I have been sent to watch over you," he said.

It was like the air had left Dray's lungs. He couldn't quite catch a breath. This man appeared different from the others, his movements smooth. Dray wasn't sure if he was man or monster.

He met Dray's stare across the flames. "You could poke me with your sword and see," he said, the slightest hiss on the edge of his voice.

"Why doesn't she just kill us?" Ed asked. Although he sounded despondent, he maintained his strong defensive stance, ready to attack if needed with his father's sword.

The man across the flames grinned, a too-wide grin that made Dray shiver. "Where would be the fun in that?"

"We need to do something she would not expect," Dray murmured.

"Is such a thing possible? I understand that she knows the soldier well. She would understand where you are going before you do."

"And yet she wasn't able to find us for so long."

"Are you certain?" the man hissed.

Ed nodded, but Dray remained still. If she had thought them a threat, she would have searched the world for them, and perhaps she had done in many ways. She wasn't linked; he couldn't tell if she was in the same room or not. She wasn't the same woman. The woman who had been Ana, or part Ana, was gone. Whatever this woman answered to, she was not the woman they thought she could be.

The man watched him silently across the flames. Dray knew that he, or it, read his mind completely—they all did. Ana was dead. The creature who sat on the throne wearing Ed's crown might resemble her, but she wasn't her and they owed her nothing.

"She is Queen. You owe her much."

"She owes us for putting her there," Ed answered, the same anger in his voice that Dray had felt at the loss of Ana. This woman was to blame. This queen had already taken too much from them.

"Do you expect to travel with us?" Dray asked.

The man stepped closer to the fire. Dray thought of how a fire would have once kept animals at bay, but those living in the darkness no longer feared the light.

"It would never be bright enough to hurt us," the man said, sitting in the grass by the fire.

"If we are not a threat, why take Belle?" Ed asked, still standing.

"You like her," he said, as though he were a friend teasing another. "She is important to you, not to Majesty."

Dray waited, trying hard to keep an open mind and just listen.

"You will act rashly to get her back. You might be side-tracked from your original plan. You might even return to Majesty."

"There is a lot of guessing from a woman who supposedly knows us so well," Ed said.

The man's smile slipped, his face darkening for the first time.

"Not quite the all-seeing queen she claims to be," Forest murmured, and a small huff of laughter left Dray's lips before he could stop it.

"She has sent her lackey to watch over us because we are a threat, because she knows we have the strength she does not." Dray smiled broadly, and the man who had settled by the fire leapt effortlessly to his feet.

"That is why she sent you," Ed said, sliding the sword back into the sheath. The three of them sat back down as one, and the boy before them turned into something tall and dark. "Will you travel with us as you are, or hide behind us in the shadows like her other creatures do?"

Dray was sure he could feel anger rolling from the creature, and then it was gone. They waited in silence before Dray breathed out. "I think we have just angered her further."

"How much light do you suppose we would need?" Ed asked. Dray looked from the space the creature had occupied to the king. "He said we would never be bright enough."

Dray nodded slowly. He had tried not to wonder at the same thing while the creature had stood so close. But without Belle and her gift, if it was a gift, they may not know. "Is that why they took Belle?" he wondered.

"Where did they take her to?" Forest asked.

"We can't dwell on that," Ed said too quickly, and although Dray was sure the king did just that, he said nothing. "We must make it to the forest. We need to reach the Near Folk, and then we can find Belle."

Dray nodded more to himself, hoping that Belle was safe and able to look after herself. He thought her capable, but he had thought the same of Ana until she had fallen into the mage's hands.

# 17

"Majesty?" the soldier asked, stepping closer than Ana was prepared for. As she lifted her eyes from the floor before her, he flinched. She closed her eyes, drinking in the fear, and sighed.

"I have had enough today," she told him. She didn't want to talk to any more people, despite the overwhelming trust that had grown throughout the castle that day. It was enough.

"The new soldiers," he stammered, and she blinked into the dim light.

"Is it night?"

He nodded slowly.

"I would eat," she said, waving him away and making no move to raise herself from the throne. She was more tired than she had expected. They had taken something from her. Although she had gained from the experience herself.

"What soldiers?" she asked. The man, almost to the door, stopped.

"Some of those who came today have joined our ranks."

She stood slowly, the effort almost painful. She stumbled as he drew closer, but she held up a hand to stop him.

"I shall send someone," he said, his confidence of earlier gone, although he did not move.

"New soldiers," she repeated.

"They have been fitted for uniforms, but it is hard to know who supports you, Majesty."

"My children will assist with that," she said, releasing her hold on the arm of the throne and hoping she would remain upright. One of them appeared beside her, fluid and strong, anger flowing from him.

"You had a job to do," she said, but she allowed the strong clawed hand to slide around her arm and hold her up.

"They laugh at your power; they challenge what and who you are."

"It is not for you to declare what I am," she snapped. Fear shot through the soldier standing before her. He might support her, would back her, but there was always the fear that he would not survive the day. She drank it in and waved away the child at her arm. "They think they are strong. Let them live with the ideal; it will do them no good in the end."

"Majesty," the child hissed, bowing smoothly, and Ana ran her hand over the child's bowed head. She saw within the creature's mind the three of them in the firelight.

"They are not what they were, nor will they be again," Ana said, her voice soothing. "Watch from a distance. Take the boy with you."

Another shadow appeared before them, forming into a wildly grinning creature. She wanted to be proud of the child before her, but there was disappointment. It had once been the lord's son, but it had been too keen to impress, too conflicted in how to do that.

"Prove yourself," she hissed, and the child bowed awkwardly.

"If they make it to the trees," the soldier said, his fear spiking as Ana turned her attention to him. "They will be safe from you."

"No one is ever safe from me." She stepped confidently forward, reenergised by the fear. She needed the people behind her; it was the only way she could truly rule as she had intended. The lack of fear had taken its toll, but it was easily replenished.

"I like this armour," she said, tapping his chest with a long fingernail. "Who did that?"

"I took the liberty, Majesty," the man said, bowing his head.

"What rank are you?"

"Is that important?"

She appeared behind him in a heartbeat. His heart beating faster, his fear filling her veins. "I asked, and therefore it is. Perhaps you should be elevated; perhaps I should find something new to call you. Queen Liaison." She rested her hand on his shoulder, and he flinched. She ran her hand down his arm and, despite his strong stance, the fear built around him. "Queen's Man—no, that is dull. Shadow Master?" The child by the throne growled. "Oh well, something appropriate will come to me, Grant." She leaned in closer to him, although he didn't appeal to her as a man. She was only interested now in what people could give her.

"In the meantime," she hissed in his ear. "See to it that all soldiers wear the new armour, whether they support me openly or not. They are my men, after all."

"Do you want us to go after the king?" His face paled as he realised the words he had used, but despite her inclination to destroy the man before her, she simply smiled and shook her head.

"I know where he is, and the last soldiers that went after him have been lost. The children can do as I need in relation to *the boy*."

He bowed low, fist thumped over his heart. As she gave him a small nod, he disappeared.

"He would be more use as a child," the child behind her said.

"Perhaps they all would. I wanted to rule this world as it was, not turn it into my own."

"Majesty."

"I sense the question, child, but do not ask it. I know what I am, and I will rule as I see fit, not you. Show me the face you showed to them."

Reluctantly, the child shifted and became a young man, tall and lean. Ana might have once considered him handsome.

"I was more than a boy beyond."

"This is a different world. If you want to raise yourself up, you must prove yourself here."

He bowed again and disappeared. She watched the threads of the shadows he had moved through long after he was gone, wondering just what he was and what he would do to prove himself to her.

Belle lay on her back, looking up at the stars twinkling in the inky black sky so far above her. She couldn't sleep. It wasn't that she worried what else might be done, for she would be at the whim of the witch no matter what she tried. It was for Ed she worried. He had Dray at his side, and the sword master, but there was something about Dray she had yet to work out. Not that he had a magic—he was just a soldier, after all—but there was something in him that sensed the magic, sensed the unknown.

It was how he managed to understand that Ana was close even when she couldn't be seen in the shadows. It was how he understood Salima saw so much, and that she was something stronger than her father. Belle would never have guessed that either of them was a dragon. Dray knew things even before he knew them. Like the need to save Ana.

She had felt his turmoil that he had caused the current state of the world by saving her, but she knew as well as he did he could never have let her fall. Ana had been just a girl, but there was something else, something else inside her. She'd had magic before that which had awoken; she had healed Ed. There was something natural in her, and yet Belle could only see the witch. The secretive, disappearing woman who had promised to help Ed and had only helped herself.

"Please stop that," the mage murmured as he rolled away from her.

She sat up and looked across at him. "I'm not doing anything."

"Are you angry, worked up?"

"Just thinking about the state of the world, and Ana."

"Angry."

She waited.

"I can see you glowing. The more worked up you get, the brighter you glow. It isn't very bright in relation to the girl, but there is potential."

"Could you help me?"

"To shine?"

Belle nodded slowly despite the dark. The fire they had built up had died away to embers. The night wasn't cold, but the mage had thought to keep the shadows away, although Belle doubted they could do very much to prevent them. Even if she glowed. Kemp had said as much, that she was nothing to scare him. "But I could be," she murmured. "If I learnt how to shine, I could be a threat to them."

"Do you really think she would have put you with me to allow that to happen?"

"I think she sees you as some useless old man clutching at straws. You found the other girl by accident, didn't really know the power she had, and when she tried to use it, Ana and her shadows destroyed it. And her," Belle added slowly. "Even if I learn to use whatever gift I have, or you think I have, I can't get close enough to do any harm."

He grumbled something that she didn't quite hear. "You don't see it," he said, clearing his throat.

She shook her head. Others around her did, but she did not herself.

"Find it first. Find the glow within, and then I will help you."

Belle lay down and turned her attention back to the stars. She had no idea how to start.

"Sleep," he murmured.

Belle closed her eyes and tried, but sleep wouldn't come. She tried to think of Ed, but the worry only made it harder. She sighed and thought of Dray, the strong soldier watching over him, despite his losses, and then it was as though they were standing in the same field. Dray opened his mouth and closed it, then turned to look over his shoulder.

Ed and Master Forest lay sleeping soundly by the fire. When Dray turned back to Belle, there was a level of fear in his eyes.

"I'm actually here," she said, turning her hand in front of her face. "I thought I was sleeping."

He nodded. "It is no longer my watch, so perhaps you are. We had a shadow here tonight, and I am sure another will come."

"Why does this worry you?" she asked stepping closer, and he backed up. "Ana visited you in your dreams."

He nodded once.

"I'm just trying to find out what I am, and I was thinking of what you might be."

"I'm just a soldier."

"I don't believe that," she said.

"You can believe what you want, but I am nothing more than a sword to protect the king."

"Do you still see Ana in your dreams?"

He looked to the ground, and she could see the same hurt she had seen when they had sat out in the field, lost in the grass, talking of what they had lost.

"Sometimes, but not as she was. Or is. It is hard to explain."

"Can you try?"

"Where are you?" he asked instead.

"On my way to the Near Forest."

"Alone?"

She took a deep breath and shook her head. "The mage," she said.

"No," Dray breathed, stepping forward and taking her by the shoulders. "You can't stay with him. He will use you like he did Ana, and you too will be lost."

"He will help me if only to help himself."

"No, Belle."

"Tell me of the dream," she said more forcefully. Her hands closed round the front of his shirt to prevent him from moving away, although his grip on her shoulders seemed to have grown tighter, as though he didn't want her to return to the mage.

"She walks from the darkness. That is it. Ana, as I knew her, walks towards me."

"You think she can be saved."

He shook his head. "I think it is my way of accepting she is gone. Our last interactions were confusing. She is here but not. The dream gives me peace, despite my not knowing what it means."

Belle nodded slowly, then looked to the side as movement caught her eye. A creature moved towards them from the shadows in a strange way. Belle imagined the Ana in Dray's dream moving the same way. But the creature's grin and its tongue scared her more than the idea of Ana for a moment, and she screamed.

Belle blinked into the early morning light, the stars above her gone and the old mage snoring quietly a short distance away.

She turned slowly to take in her surroundings, hoping that the creature hadn't followed her here, or that it wasn't here rather than in the dream. She found no sign of any creatures, not that it meant they weren't here somewhere, hiding amongst the strange morning shadows. She nudged at the sleeping mage with her foot, and he snorted before waking and sitting up with a start.

"What?" he asked, wiping the sleep from his eyes.

"I thought I saw something in the shadows."

He got to his feet, looking around the trees, and then turned with a sigh to look out over the fields that surrounded them. "We may never know if they are with us or not."

"True," she murmured, climbing to her feet and brushing at her skirt. It would have been nice if the monsters who had stolen her away had managed to bring the bag she had been carrying as well. "I was just worried. I'm used to better protection of a night than a sleeping mage."

"Will Ana come for us?" he asked, looking back at her. "She gave you to me, and she knows very well where I am headed. If she had wanted either of us, we would be at the castle, the capital or anywhere else she might decide."

"She did not give me to you," Belle murmured. "She was removing me from my friends. She is playing games leaving us in the middle of nowhere." Just like the others were, in a field somewhere between the grasslands and the forest. If they still had the horses, they were much closer to the forest, or at least they would reach it sooner.

The mage straightened his coat and then looked back over the fields beyond the small group of trees before walking towards the road.

"Do you know where you are going?" she asked, and he shrugged. "Are we to blindly follow the road?"

"It is how the boy… king," he corrected, bowing his head to her, "made it so far. He just followed the road."

"He at least had a goal."

"You don't think I have a plan?" he asked incredulously.

"Do you?"

"Forest, king, way to defeat the witch."

"Sounds like a plan. Possibly similar to our plan, although we already had the king. It is the defeat part that seems to be the sticking point of any plan."

"But you have a plan," he said, turning back to her, a silver eyebrow raised. Although she knew he had slept in his clothes, he appeared to be just as he always had been. When she didn't respond, he continued, "You will find a way to shine and destroy the shadows."

"I'm not even sure I do shine."

"Maybe you should have looked for a dragon while you were in the mountains, but I suppose you didn't need one then."

"A dragon," Belle said slowly, trying not to smile.

"They may be able to show you the light, or produce it on their own. I have never met one myself, but I have heard of their fire."

"Fire?" she asked.

"It is all myth, of course," the mage went on, making his way slowly along the road with Belle at his side. "I assume they would have the ability to breathe flames, like the stories of old."

"If that were the case, we might have lit the shadows and destroyed them long before you had to find your little girl."

He sighed and continued in silence. "It might be easier than we hoped."

"Then why haven't we been able to stop her?" Belle demanded.

He sighed again. "That, child, might be because the people with the skills to stop her chose not to."

# 18

Ed literally jumped out of his skin as Dray sat up shouting. The morning light had started to spread across the landscape and, despite all that was going on around them, he thought it beautiful and wanted to share that with Belle.

Forest leapt as well, only he managed not to scream.

Dray sucked in a large breath, looked around and then focused on Ed. "Sorry," he muttered. "Dream."

"Of Ana?" Ed asked before he could stop himself.

Dray shook his head and climbed to his feet. He glanced around again and then at the horses tethered not far from the fire. Ed wasn't sure if they would startle. They had seemed to be fine so far. Even when the creatures had surrounded them, the horses had not shown signs of distress. He wondered then how many shadows they had been around, and for how long. His mind raced with the possibilities. How many were around the lord? How many were around the kingdom? How many might watch their every move?

"Did you see one?" Ed asked.

Dray shook his head and then nodded. "I think it was a dream," he said again.

"What did you see?" Forest asked.

"Belle," he murmured, then looked at Ed. "A creature."

"Was Belle the creature?" Ed asked, a mad idea forming in his mind that Ana had stolen her to turn her into another shadow monster. She was a threat, after all, or at least she might be if she worked out the shining thing.

"Belle is with the mage," he said.

"You are sure?"

"She found a way to reach me," he said, his voice apologetic, and Ed felt the burn of jealousy.

"What magic do you have?" Ed blurted. He didn't want to get angry with Dray; it was news, and it was good news. Or at least better than he'd feared. If Belle had been able to reach him, she would have. She would always try to reach him first.

Dray shook his head.

"Is there something that draws them to you?"

"Ed," Forest interrupted, "I don't think that is what it is."

"It is something, something we haven't been able to explain."

Dray walked towards his horse and pulled something from his bag. Then he was rolling his bed roll. Ed looked over the four horses and realised they still carried Belle's bag. "Can we give it back?" he asked.

"We are all headed to the same place; you can check on her then."

"Are they close?"

Dray shook his head.

"I understand that we need to make it to Near Forest. That we have a better chance of being safe there and getting the support we need to end this." Ed tried to remain calm, but there was a panic in his chest he couldn't explain.

Dray looked up from the bed roll, but said nothing.

"I want to find her," Ed blurted.

"We will find each other," Dray said, standing slowly. "We will come together. The time apart, although not what we wanted, might be what we need."

Ed shook his head.

"She is safe; she told me so. We don't know where they are. This is why she separated us," he said more firmly. "This is why

Ana does what she does. It is a game, and one she thinks will push us off course. She wants you focused on Belle and where she might be rather than what we need to do."

Ed sighed and looked at his feet. Dray was right; he was always right. All of this was difficult enough. They barely had any support. They were begging for it from those who already feared. And Ana seemed to be working on not just ruling with fear. He nodded slowly. And when he looked up, Dray gave him a nod in return.

Forest was already pushing dirt over the dying fire and striding towards his horse. "I understand," he said softly as he climbed up onto the large beast. "If I could have followed Salima, I would have. But we have work to do."

"She will find us," Dray assured him.

"I would rather she stay out of this," Forest murmured, "but I know she won't. She will do what she can to help Ed."

"I don't want her hurt, and if I could keep her safe I would. But she is a dragon and something very different from what we both thought," Ed said, climbing onto his horse.

"That doesn't make it any easier. I thought I was keeping her safe for a different reason. I thought…" Forest shook his head and kicked his horse into action.

Ed watched him ride ahead for a moment, and then they were all moving much faster than Ed had thought he would be able to on a horse—and, he hoped, headed north. He tried to watch the road ahead and visualise the forest waiting for them, ready to protect them and help them find a way, but he couldn't. He watched over his shoulder, twisting in the saddle to check the world around them. He was certain the shadows followed them, and that there was more around them than fields and abandoned houses.

As they passed another farm, he thought he saw someone at a window. In all the travelling they had done, he had seen so few people. He wondered if the people hid when they heard them coming, or if they simply hid. The world was not as it had been.

Not for the first time, he wondered if he would be worthy of these people. If he had the ability to rule any better than those who had come before him. At least he hoped he would not rule with fear as Ana did, nor with selfishness as his uncle had.

The horse stumbled beneath him, and he looked ahead to a shadow on the road. He tried to hang on as he allowed the horse to find its feet. But as they got closer, the shadow dissipated. The horse whinnied as the three of them slowed.

"Did you see that?" Ed asked the others.

"I just saw you slow," Forest said, looking around them.

"They are with us, the shadows. I think she just wants to let us know we can't win this." Any hope of his sitting on the throne seemed to be slipping away.

"Do you want to give up?" Dray asked. Ed turned to take in his serious features, his confident posture on the horse, then shook his head. The soldier smiled at Ed and nudged his horse forward. "Prove it," he muttered as he led the way along the road.

Ed hoped the shadows weren't going to keep appearing out of nowhere. He couldn't focus on that; he had to focus on what they needed to do and not let Ana get to him. He was King, after all—it was about time he started to behave like one. As they pushed their horses on, he tried to ignore the lack of people, the fear he could almost sense in the air and the shadows he thought moved around him.

At one point he was sure he saw a shadow by the road, and as they drew closer it formed into the man who had appeared at their fire. Dray drew his sword, but the man disappeared before they reached him.

Dray growled something under his breath and then urged his horse on faster. Ed wasn't sure they would last the distance. They were moving faster than he expected, yet they were still in the grasslands. He had walked across much of the kingdom, after all, and he knew it was going to take them too long to reach friends. He gulped down his fear of what Belle might be doing and whom she might be with.

"The mage," he murmured. Dray looked back over his shoulder. "Where are they?"

Dray's focus returned to the road and, as he leaned forward to pat the horse's neck, Ed realised just how low the light was. Had they been riding at this rate all day?

"I think we need to stop," he said.

It was Master Forest who shook his head. Although Ed didn't want to allow any distance to come between them, he slowed.

"We can't," Forest called back. Dray reached out for his horse, and then the two of them drew in closer together and slowed to a stop as Ed allowed his horse to walk forward.

"I am just as desperate to reach the trees," Ed admitted, "but we can't continue at this pace. We need to let the horses rest, and I need to stretch my legs and eat."

"Agreed," Dray said, his hand still on Forest's horse.

Ed climbed down from the animal, looking around for a place they could camp. Again, the side of the road appeared to be their only option. The horse beside him started to prance. "Shh," he whispered. He held the reins tightly in one hand as he patted the horse's neck with the other, but it moved around all the more and then reared up.

Ed searched the surrounding area but found nothing. The horses hadn't shied when the shadows had appeared before. What might it be that would scare them? The horse raced forward, pulling the reins from his hand, and he cried out as it took off.

"I'll go after it," Forest offered as the horse disappeared into the night.

"And then we'll lose you both," Dray muttered, his hand still on the sword master's mount. "I can't risk you."

The man sighed and nodded once.

"Will it come back?" Ed asked hopefully.

Dray shook his head as he climbed down from his horse, his hand tight on the reins. It didn't appear spooked. Ed wondered again if a shadow could have done this. As Dray reached Ed, his hand resting reassuringly on his shoulder, the sword master took off at a full gallop.

Dray growled, but Ed shook his head. "Let him go," he said. "We need to work together, and we can't spend our time just trying to keep him with us. He will work it out. I trust him."

"As do I," Dray said. "It is others I don't trust. Where will he go?"

"The trees. Salima." Ed looked around the small space surrounding them as the sun dipped beneath the horizon. "We will find each other."

Dray looked at him seriously. "I know I said the same; we are all headed to the trees. But what if this is another way to separate us? What if we are all headed in different directions?"

"You can't doubt," Ed said, panic closing in around his chest. "You are the only one amongst us with any real faith that we can sort this out. If you don't think we can do it, we can't."

Dray sighed. "I want to believe we can do this," he said. "But I must admit I'm struggling."

Ed nodded slowly.

"I spent so much time sure that Salima would find us, reassuring Forest that she would come. But it has been months, and she hasn't."

Ed smiled at the idea. "You were the one who was so sure she would find us when the time was right. The time isn't right yet. Salima is far more than I expected her to be," he said quietly, looking up at the faint stars starting to shine more brightly in the darkening sky. "She will do as she promised."

"Will she?" a voice hissed in the dark.

"I know my sister," Ed called into the dark.

"Do you?" it hissed closer. Ed was sure he could feel a breath, or a dry tongue, touch across his skin. It took all he had not to shiver. "I know your fear."

"As do I," Ed said, turning to face the voice to find there was nothing there. No creature. The shadows lost in the darkness. He looked back at Dray and then at the horse. Maybe he was right; maybe they didn't have a chance.

The shadows cackled, and silence followed.

"Do you think it is still around?" he asked. "Or does it come and go?"

"I don't think we could ever know. I'll start a fire. Let's eat, rest for a short while and see if we can catch Forest."

"Agreed," Ed said, but he looked around the field in the dying light and wondered if the creatures were that far away.

For the first time in a long time, Dray dreamt of Ana. It was the simple dream of her walking from the darkness. Yet it scared him, as though there was no hope of her walking to him, as though he would never find her in the dark. She wore the same dress she had the day he had pulled her from the Walk. He looked up into the dark sky at the distant stars, listening to the movement of the horse, and tried to remind himself of where he was. He sat up and looked towards where he had tethered the horse, grateful it was still there.

It was odd that the king's horse had been spooked. The animals seemed to be able to cope with anything, including the long hours of riding. Even being surrounded by shadows. He couldn't imagine what it might have been. Then something moved amidst the darkness, a deeper dark, and the horse moved around again.

Something was scaring them. Dray was on his feet, his hand on the reins before the animal could hurt itself. It was prancing about, tugging at the bonds, and as Dray tried to calm the animal it swung a head towards him. The light of the fire disappeared. As they stood together, the horse becoming more agitated, Dray felt the hair stand on the back of his neck and arms. There was something out there, not very far away.

His heart leapt in his chest as a hand rested on his shoulder.

"What is going on?" Ed whispered, leaning in close.

"I don't know, but I don't like it."

The horse reared up again, this time tugging the reins free of the tree, and Dray's only thought was that something had loosened or released them. The leather pulled through his hands, and the horse was gone.

They stood in the dark silence and listened, Ed's hand still on his shoulder. Dray wasn't sure whom that was to offer comfort to, but it was reassuring that they were together. There was no sound of the horse, no distant sound of hoof beats. It had gone, disappeared.

"Are they taking horses now?" he asked. "Are they creating different monsters?"

Ed remained silent.

"Your Majesty," Dray ventured.

"I'm still here," Ed said, and Dray sucked in a relieved breath. "I'm trying to work out what is going on and what we do next. Only I have no idea."

# 19

Ana looked over the horses in the courtyard and wondered what they were doing. They had been there all night. She had heard them at some point during the night, but now they stood in silence as though scared of what else might happen.

"Why?" she asked.

"I thought it funny, Majesty," the boy hissed, his grin too wide. Not for the first time, she wondered if it had been a good idea to make the lord's son one of hers.

"Funny?" she asked, allowing the darkness to echo around the courtyard. The boy didn't even flinch.

"That Ed guy was so scared, I could taste it." He licked his lips, and Ana tried not to sigh. "The soldier was even funnier. So strong and sure. No amount of speed with a sword could save him from that."

Ana growled. "You are to do as you are directed."

The boy looked at her, his grin still wide. "I did."

"You did not," she hissed, anger growing at his lack of respect. "Teach him," she called, and another child appeared before her.

"How would you have me instruct him, Majesty?" the child asked with a bow.

"As you see fit—and get these animals out of here."

The child bowed low, and Ana ran her hand over the back of its head before she stomped back to the throne room. The boy was supposed to be a way for her to get to the lord, not to take petty revenge like a child.

Although, she had to admit it would be worthwhile to see them try to survive without their horses.

"The sword master has left them," a child hissed as she sat back in the throne.

"Truly?"

"He wanted to reach the dragon."

"She isn't in the forest," Ana said, studying the child before her.

"We are not sure where," he hissed.

"Find out," she snapped. "Leave the sword master. Watch him, but don't interfere. I doubt the man can do very much on his own."

The child bowed and disappeared. The soldier by the door cleared his throat.

"Majesty." He bowed low when she gave him her attention. "There are those who would talk with you."

She shook her head. She wanted to rule—she wanted to be as powerful as those who had come before—but she couldn't face another day of talking to the people, sorting out their issues and listening to their woes. She had managed to strengthen her army and her children with the last day, but she didn't have the strength to do it again so soon.

"Seven days," she said.

"Majesty?" he asked, his fear evident at questioning her.

"I will see them and listen to them every seven days. Has it been that long?"

He shook his head.

"Grant," she said kindly, standing. He flinched before stepping forward to meet her. "You are a clever man. And I am yet to find you a title."

"Captain is enough," he said.

She growled, and he stepped back.

"I will find you another," she said. "Tell the people I will see them on the seventh day."

He bowed and backed out of the room. She could taste the fear that followed him. There was a sense of pride, but she enjoyed that he still felt some fear. It meant that he was more likely to do as he was told.

Ruth appeared before her, bowing her head low. "What would you have me do?"

"I wish I had more like you. Belle is being watched?"

Ruth bowed her head. Kemp had been sent after her, and she knew they travelled slowly. But Ana wanted some fun with them. The old man was too confident that he could outsmart her. She now watched the king and any who might assist him, although she wished she could see the dragons better. They were somewhere in the Dry, and she found it frustrating that she couldn't reach them with certainty.

"The lords do as directed," she murmured.

"Not all of them," Ruth said.

When Ana looked up, the girl hung her head.

"Tell me," Ana said.

"They think of the king."

"The boy said the Lord of the Grassland sent him away, would not help him."

"He prepares for something."

Ana sighed. Why was no one doing as they should? "Watch them."

The girl nodded and disappeared. She could place Ruth wherever she needed her and, if needed, she could place the son or a replica back before the lord. He was old school; he understood how the world worked. Ana was sure he would be what they needed, a loyal man directing his province to continue to provide for the kingdom as it had.

Ana blinked into the sword master's practice halls to find a number of soldiers in practice swordplay. At the sight of her, they stopped, turned as one and bowed. They did not raise their fists, but then they all had swords. She nodded her head, and they returned to what they had been doing. She moved amongst them, looking over men she would not otherwise know. If the world had been different and another soldier had saved her from the Walk, would Dray be here amongst these men, proving his loyalty?

It didn't matter. She had two armies. She sensed a nervousness from some, open fear from others as she moved around the room. It had been so long since she had been in here, and the windows illuminated the entire space with morning sunshine. Several of her children waited in the shadows, always watching, ensuring the soldiers were doing as she needed them to.

She gave them permission to leave. These men were loyal, she could taste it. She closed her eyes, drank it in and blinked back to her balcony to look over a kingdom that felt different from what it had been. She felt a certainty. Still some fear and disappointment, but she knew they would follow her. Even if they didn't want to, they would see it as best for the kingdom.

Ana was finally starting to feel like she was where she was meant to be. Like this world would be hers after all. She blinked back to the throne room, the cold stone of the throne comfortable and solid beneath her. Children appeared before her, each holding a citizen of her city, of her kingdom, who wanted their boy king back on the throne.

Some dropped to their knees. Others fought against the hold of the children, whose sharp claws prevented them from escaping.

"I will not have this," she growled, standing. The movement in the room stopped. "I am your queen."

"Never!" one man spat. "You stole the crown."

"I did no such thing," Ana hummed, stepping closer as he writhed in the hold of the child. She ran a fingernail down the side of his face, leaving a thick red mark in its wake. "He gave it to me. The boy did not want to be King."

"Lies," the man spat, and she wiped a hand over her face. The child behind him growled. She held up a hand before it could kill him. "You stole it from him. You persuaded him. He needed help and guidance and you took advantage of that, just as his uncle did. He will be King."

"Are you even sure he is alive?" she asked, looking down the line of citizens. They looked to the man before her, and he nodded once. Confident in the boy.

"We will find a way to defeat you and put him on the throne."

Ana laughed. Stepping back, she allowed the sound to fill the room. "You have no chance against me and my children. We are far too strong, and we have the support of most of the kingdom."

"No," the man said, "you don't."

"I can help you, Majesty," a child said, appearing too close to the throne behind her. Before she had a chance to say a word—and although he knew he was not to act—the child consumed the man.

"No," she growled. "Lock them away," she instructed. The other children disappeared as the men who had been standing in her throne room began to shout and scream and fight.

The boy who had once been the son of a lord grinned. Ana wondered if the problem was the boy himself or the shadow she had linked to him to create the child. He had been weak as a boy, too keen to please, but as a child he was rash and impulsive and did not follow instructions.

Another child appeared before her, bowing low. Another that had bound with two and yet was something very different from the grinning fool before her. "You were under instruction."

"I didn't need it," he hissed, stepping closer to the throne.

"You need to be reminded who is Queen."

"Do I?" He staggered, the already awkward movements made more so as his long legs crashed into the hard stone floor of the throne room. His wild grin disappeared, and Ana took a step closer. His hands flew to his throat, a strangled cry escaping his lips as a dark, thick liquid oozed from the corner of his mouth.

The man inside him was fighting back; Ana could feel it. They were still separate. The child thought himself stronger than he was, and he had no real idea of what he was. The struggle continued as Ana watched with interest.

*He can't break free.*

"No," Ana whispered. "They are separate, and yet as long as the shadow remains it cannot be two."

*The child was already one. We must punish them. Both of them.*

Ana nodded once and, with a slicing motion of her hand, the child before her stopped struggling and fell in a heap on the floor. Despite the darkness she felt, the struggle continued. Ana took a deep breath, disappointed that it had come to this. She needed all the help she could get. She focused on the darkness within the near lifeless being before her and squeezed it free. The shadows disappeared before her, and two remained.

The man who had just been consumed looked up at her. "You cannot win," she whispered, leaning down over him, yet he smiled before the last of his life slipped from him.

The other boy was already dead. He looked even younger, and she was disappointed that he had not become what she had needed him to.

She looked up at the child still standing at the edge of the scene. "You were to train him, educate him."

"The boy inside was too strong, too determined to create trouble. He was jealous and hateful and wilful. He would not listen."

"It doesn't matter now, but he has interfered where I wished he had not."

"The other boy is not worth the time. These men will not help him. They will not be able to defeat us. They must learn to work with us for the kingdom or die."

"My thought exactly, child. But for now, leave the others in the cells. See if that will not help them remember who their queen is."

"Majesty." The child bowed low before her.

"Send someone to clean this up; a soldier or the like would do." Ana sat back down on the throne and, in the following silence, wondered if she could control the world as she thought she could.

*They are nothing but pawns.*

Ana tapped at the armrest as she nodded, but she wondered if that was enough.

# 20

"I can't do this!" Belle screamed. The frustration was overwhelming. It didn't matter what she tried, how she tried it, or what advice the mage gave—she was not glowing.

"You are already doing it!" he growled back, just as frustrated that she couldn't seem to work out how to find the magic within her.

"It isn't what I am," she said. "I can sense things, I can feel things, but I can't glow."

"You have something special. More girls than you would realise can sense the world around them. It is what they do with that sense that makes the magic."

"Makes the magic?" She sighed and sat down on the cool grass. "You are just making this up. What did the other girl do?"

"I'm not sure," he admitted, rubbing a hand through his mussy hair as he sat down beside her. "I couldn't really see it. I could see it but not understand it, and then there was a spark and she hit a shadow creature with light."

"She didn't harm it," Belle said.

"She did some damage, or at least startled it, and it disappeared. You saw her in the room, before they took the magic away from her. She shone. She lit up the world and did some damage then."

"Not to Ana," Belle whispered. "Not enough to hurt her."

"But you will," he reassured.

"I can't. I can't see it."

He ran his hand through his hair again and leaned back in the grass, eyes closed.

"You don't know how to make this happen," she said. "You are so determined that this is possible, yet you don't know."

"I guide people to magic," he said, his eyes still closed, his hands across his chest. "I help many find what they are, or I use them for the magic they have."

Belle waited, but he didn't look up or give any hint that he might be joking. She wondered just what other atrocities he had been involved in. He was a man who worked for himself, to do what he could to better his place in the world, whether that meant working for someone else or against them. And it would change in an instant if he thought it would better his situation.

"Why did you want me?" she asked.

"I saw the magic glow. I knew you were strong."

"You wanted to use me."

He nodded.

"But you don't know how to make me work. It is like owning a lamp but not having any oil."

He looked up and rolled to one side to prop himself up on an elbow. He studied her, and she him in return. "You may have something there."

"But does it help? Can you find the oil?"

"You will need to find the oil. It is more of a case that if the lamp wants to shine, it will find the fuel."

She growled out her frustrations. This man wasn't going to help her at all. He shielded his eyes and leaned back. "You can't even see me," she said, leaping to her feet. "You keep telling me I'm shining, but I'm not. You can't see it. You only want to see it, and it may be that I don't shine at all."

"Am I the only one who mentioned you shining?" the mage asked, sitting up and watching her pace back and forth.

"Ana. Kemp. Do you think they would lie to you about such a

thing?" She stopped pacing. "I saw it when you first appeared in the throne room, when the king thought he could appeal to his uncle. When you should have been tribute."

She stared at him. That was the first time Ana had moved her with the shadows. She had never been more scared, not even when she'd been faced with a group of men dragging her away from her family home.

"That was why she took me," she said, finally understanding what Ana had saved her from.

"I think she might have been your friend then. She saw the same thing I did, and she knew I would use you."

"As you are trying to do now."

"I am trying to help you," he said, climbing slowly to his feet. "But you need to find it first."

Something moved behind him, and she looked beyond him as he swung around. There was nothing there, yet she was sure there had been. She had become too relaxed, forgetting that the shadows listened to every word, watched every move. They had tried to stay out in the direct sunlight as much as possible to try and prevent them sneaking up, but they were never truly safe.

"Did you see something?" the mage asked, looking around the field.

"I don't know," Belle said, heading towards the road. "I don't know anything anymore, other than we need to reach the forest."

"There is more to this than the forest," he said.

"No there isn't," she said, turning back to him standing in the grass. "We need to reach Ed. If I can help him, great—but chances are I won't be able to, and I'll have to use my other senses to help."

"You can't face those monsters with a strong sense of emotions. It isn't enough."

"And what skill do you bring to this?" she asked, turning away from him and walking along the road. They were travelling so slowly, she doubted they would ever reach the forest. And now they had stopped in the sunshine to work on a magic she didn't really think she had. Others might have talked about it, and Ana had even threatened her to stop it, yet she didn't understand what she did to make it happen.

She looked over her hand, trying to see something, anything, that would indicate what she was. Belle longed for Salima then, the girl she hardly knew who was a dragon and had seen something in her too. Dray had said that much, although Belle didn't think Dray had seen her shine. He had seen something, but she wasn't clear on what he was either.

"What is Dray?" she asked, turning back to the mage walking slowly along the road behind her.

"The soldier?" He shrugged, stopping to think about the question, and she grumbled under her breath that he took so many opportunities to stop. "He's a soldier."

"Yes," she grumbled, but he was far more than that.

"What do you think he is?" the mage asked, much closer behind her than she realised and she jumped with surprise.

She took a breath and shrugged, not wanting to share her ideas with him when he would likely just use them against her later. She wasn't even sure the mage wasn't here working with Ana.

"You can trust me," he said as though reading her thoughts.

She walked on without glancing back. "We need to reach the forest."

They continued in silence, Belle's mind racing with the possibilities of what she might be, what Dray was, when the dragons might return—all while trying not to think of Ed and worry about what might have happened to him. He was still with Dray; she was sure of that. She hadn't visited him again. She was tempted to try, but he had been so spooked by the experience. He at least knew she was safe, and he could let Ed and Forest know they were all headed in the same direction. She had to believe that they were.

They just had to reach the Near Folk. She glanced over her

shoulder at the slow-moving mage and wondered if they were ever going to reach the forest. Not for the first time, she considered leaving him behind. She was a much faster walker, and although they had no real supplies other than his water skin, she was safer remaining with him. Either way, the shadows could appear at any time and move her far away, back to the capital or back to the mage, if she were to leave him.

Perhaps the mage was working with Ana after all, and that was why she had been presented to him. Removed from Ed and given to the man who had wanted her all along. Ana might have saved her from him in the past, but she would not be too willing to save her now. In fact, if Belle was any sort of threat, Ana was certainly trying to destroy her.

Belle was certain she wasn't a threat; she wasn't someone who could do any sort of harm to Ana or her shadows. She just wanted to get to the forest and Eilke. They would know what to do. They would understand how best to help Ed. They would know what Ana was, what she could do and how to destroy her.

The mage puffed as he walked, appearing to work hard to keep up with Belle after catching her up. She continued as though he weren't there. He would have to find a way to keep up with her; she couldn't keep walking so slowly for him.

When they stopped that evening to make camp, Belle felt they had finally covered some ground. She hadn't given in to the mage. She had hardly talked to him for the rest of the day, and she had walked as fast as her legs would allow. At times he had fallen behind, but he had managed to keep up with her for most of the way. When they sat down that night, Belle thought they might reach the forest before winter set in, and her feet hurt far more than she'd thought they could.

She pulled her shoes free and rubbed around the tender parts on her heel. She was reminded of Ana then, and Ed's wound she had managed to heal when Belle had failed to take care of it. "She had magic before all this," Belle said.

The mage nodded slowly.

"Was it the same? Was it always dark?" She turned to him, suddenly wondering if the wound in Ed's shoulder might open up or was quietly festering beneath the skin. She had run her hand over that very spot and felt nothing, sensed nothing within it. But she had no real idea of what Ana was capable of.

"You want to return to him."

"Of course I do," she snapped. "I'm not here with you by choice. I was dragged here just to upset the balance of things, to unsettle us."

"You seem more angry than unsettled," the mage said, leaning back.

"Don't start your useless talk again. I am not glowing."

"No, you're not," a voice hissed from the darkness surrounding the fire.

Belle closed her eyes and took a deep breath. She wasn't going to be scared; she couldn't be scared all the time. It wouldn't get them anywhere.

"But you are scared," the voice hissed close in her ear, and she was sure she felt a dry tongue touch her face.

"Yes," she admitted, "I am. But not enough to give up. So you can tell that woman, the witch who sits in her castle pretending the world loves her, that she is nothing. She is certainly no queen."

"You can tell her yourself," it hissed. Belle felt the cold shadows pull around her, and then she was standing before Ana on her throne. The creature pushed her forward, and she stumbled and fell to her knees.

"What is this?" Ana asked, all sweetness, as though she weren't surprised that Belle had appeared before her.

"Still sending others to do your work?" Belle asked.

Ana scowled as Belle climbed to her feet. Feeling a little shaky from the journey, she brushed her tattered, dirty skirt.

"I suppose you want a new one," Ana said, and the skirt was replaced as she had done for Belle long ago. "Or do you see yourself as Queen?" The new skirt was replaced with a lush dress Belle could never imagine wearing. She ran her hands slowly down over the material, then looked up at Ana.

"You aren't dressed as a queen," Belle said.

"I dress how I please." Ana stood and stepped down to meet Belle, her perfect green dress showing just how beautiful a woman she was. Yet it differed from the thin black dresses she had worn beneath the cloak.

"Others dressed me then," Ana said.

"The cloak?" Belle asked.

Ana growled and Belle stepped back, almost falling at the force of the sound. The beast behind her took her arm and stopped her.

"You dragged her here to talk about clothes?" Ana asked of the beast.

"She thinks you are a pretender."

"Is that so?" Ana asked. Her green eyes glowed dangerously as Belle nodded slowly. "And what will you do?"

"Find a way." Belle stood taller, despite the fear that seemed to be increasing in her chest and the grin on Ana's face as it did.

"You could always shine," Ana laughed.

"She can't," the beast behind her hissed.

Belle let her frustration build, her anger at the situation, but she didn't see anything, and Ana only laughed all the more.

"Poor little Belle. Still not living up to me. Still being outshined." She laughed again.

"What will you do?" Belle asked.

"I'm not sure," Ana said, looking her over. "Maybe I can lock you away. Oh," she said, a smile spreading across her face that reminded Belle of the shadow creatures. "I have just the place."

"What of the mage?" Belle asked quickly.

"Useless old man. Let him think he is working out a way to defeat me; we will watch him." She nodded to the creature behind her, which let her go and bowed before it disappeared.

"What will you do now that you don't have one of your

creatures to do your work?"

"I'll do it myself," Ana said, stepping forward as Belle backed up. But Ana grabbed her arm before Belle could step out of her reach, and then they were standing in another room. The sun streamed in through the long narrow windows. "I may return with food," Ana said before disappearing.

Belle looked around the room and stepped up to one of the windows to look out over the city below. They were somewhere in the castle.

She turned to the small table and chair and ran her finger along the mantle. It was covered in dust apart from another line like the one her finger had made. She wondered who else had visited this room. The room was neat and self-contained, with a small bed sitting against the opposite wall. There was a pot over the fire, but it had been a long time since it had been lit, and the pot was dry and dusty. Belle sat at the small table and looked over the room, then realised there was no door.

She leapt to her feet and ran her hand over the wall. Desperation sucked the air from her lungs. There was no sign of any opening at all. She tried to calm her fears, reached out her senses and, leaning against the wall with her eyes closed, searched for a way out. There wasn't one.

She sank down to the floor, leaned her head forward into her knees and cried. She wasn't going to be able to help Ed from here.

# 21

Barlow watched the people move around the camp. His own men had made more conversation with them the longer they remained close, but they still kept their distance from him as though he might not be safe. He wasn't sure what he was doing anymore. He wasn't of use to his king; he wasn't of use to the kingdom. The Lord of Near Forest didn't really want him around. Barlow was beginning to think he would be staying here, in hiding, for the rest of his life.

The morning light pushed through the leaves. The women talked amongst themselves as they worked. The men were quieter, appearing to be more watchful. For the first time, Barlow wondered if they weren't as safe amongst the trees as he had hoped. He thought they were all hiding, that the Near Folk were keeping them safe, and yet they were just as nervous as he was.

When Eilke appeared beside him, he wasn't sure what to say. He looked up at the man, who gave him a single nod. He stood slowly and ran his hand through his hair, which appeared to have grown significantly in the days they had been in the forest. Or had it been longer than that? He was starting to lose track, and that was what was contributing to the idea that he would be here forever.

The man turned slowly and walked away. Barlow followed, silent so as not to spook the man. Not that he thought the man easily spooked, but it had taken some time before Eilke would trust him, although he wasn't sure what he was being trusted with.

They walked one after the other through the trees and then stopped, the breath leaving Barlow's lungs at the sight before him. There was a whole village, and the noise of people going about their morning business surprised him.

"This was just here."

"It has always been here," Eilke said, walking into the village along the main path. Although he didn't see horses or carts, Barlow thought it wide enough to be a street in the capital. Some people watched him as he walked by, women and men trying to go about their business, but the children looked and pointed. One even ran up to him and touched his sword before running away again to the cheers of his friends.

"You don't see many visitors," Barlow said.

"We see enough," Eilke responded, stopping before a building in the fork of the road. "The chief will see you."

Barlow tried to brush his wayward hair behind his ears, rubbed a sleeve over the dull armour of his breast plate and headed into the building. There was no one there but a long table, a tall chair at the other end and strange lights that drew his eye upwards. It was as though the stars still shone and this building hadn't reached the morning yet. When he looked back, an older man was sitting in the chair at the end of the table. Barlow bowed before him.

"You are a captain, like the other one."

"Dray was here?" The man waited, and Barlow nodded.

"You are searching for your king."

"I thought he would come to you. Find a safe place amongst the trees."

"He may come yet. You may wait."

"Here?" Barlow asked.

The man smiled and indicated the bench seat that ran alongside the table. Barlow sat and, locking his fingers to prevent fidgeting, he set them on the table. Dray would know how to behave, but when he was here he was most likely standing behind the king.

"Do you know who we are?"

Barlow nodded again.

"Do you know who you are?"

"At this stage, I fear I am just trying to survive. I hope to be a help to my king."

"There are few King's Men left," the chief said, and Barlow could hear the sadness in his voice.

"She promises much but delivers little. They will see her for what she is."

"It may be too late."

"Can you help us?"

"I already do. Watch the lord; he will watch the people. Others will come."

"Others to help?"

"Some," the man said cryptically, and Barlow did his best not to sigh. "Stay with us, eat with us." Although it sounded like an offer, Barlow knew it was a test of sorts.

"Will you fight with us if it comes to that?" He knew it would. It was the only way.

"We will do as we must to end the darkness."

"Will we succeed?" Barlow asked.

"I cannot see the future, Captain. It will be as it will be."

Barlow had spent too much time around people who could see so much and create from magic what they couldn't. He nodded and stood slowly. "I will return to the forest people, see how I might help them."

The chief nodded once, and the twinkling of the stars drew his attention. When he looked back, the man was gone, and when he turned for the door Eilke was waiting. Without a word, he led Barlow through the village and out through the trees until they were back in the forest with the lord and his people.

The lord looked around from his place by the fire, and Barlow gave him a nod. He didn't know how much time they had, but he didn't think it would be long before the darkness found its way to the forest.

Salima stretched and sat up as disappointment washed across her. It was time, and she wasn't ready. She wasn't even close to ready. As she looked across at Ende standing at the edge of the cliff, she knew it wouldn't matter how much time she thought she had—she wasn't ready for what came next.

Ende turned and smiled then, and she raced forward, turning into the girl he had known at the castle and throwing her arms around him. He squeezed her just as tight in return, kissing the top of her head.

"I know this will be hard," he whispered. "I have done this before. I have used my strength against others. It is not easy, but it is what must be done."

She nodded slowly against his chest, sucking as much heat from him as she could and then passing it back. He would need all he had for this and more. As would she, she realised.

"We must go to the capital," she whispered.

"Is Ed at the capital?"

She shook her head. "There is something else we must collect from there."

He looked at her quizzically. "Will this alert her?"

"She already knows where we are and that we will return. There are others who do not know or do not believe in us. But those who need to do."

"I don't want to risk you," Ende said, holding her tighter.

"But we knew it was coming, for both of us."

He sighed and let her go, giving her one final nod, and she hoped the tears she was trying to keep at bay were hidden from him.

"It is time," she repeated, stepping off the cliff and changing instantly into her dragon form. As she pushed upward on strong wings, she heard and felt her father behind her. The same strength contained in an even larger dragon. Salima hoped the fuzzy parts of the future that lay out before her were not as dark as the clarity she found in others.

# 22

As they rounded a corner in the road, Dray was surprised that Forest walked ahead of them. Not walked, limped. He looked to be dragging himself to the edge. He was clearly injured, the horse gone, his gait slow and laboured. Dray had seen similar behaviour during his time as a soldier, men wounded beyond repair but still walking, determined not to die on the battlefield.

Then Forest collapsed on the road, and they raced forward to help him up. The road passed through a small track of trees whose shade was comforting after the hot sun.

"What happened?" Ed asked, and the older man shook his head.

Dray almost picked him up, carried him off the road and sat him down in the shade of the trees. The man looked around wildly, as though there was something in the shade with them. There likely was, but the shadows would follow wherever they went. It did no good to focus on what they couldn't change.

Dray put his hand on Forest's shoulders, and he looked up with startled eyes as though just understanding that they were there.

"Where is the horse?" Ed asked slowly. Forest flinched and looked around at Ed.

He opened his mouth and then closed it.

"Forest," Dray said softly, drawing the man's attention back to him.

"It disappeared beneath me," Forest whispered, his voice dry as though he'd had nothing to drink for days. It might be that he hadn't stopped to drink or eat while racing away from them.

"Beneath you?" Ed asked, glancing at Dray.

"I was riding," he croaked. "It just disappeared. I fell heavily." He indicated his foot. Dray noticed then that his face was scratched, as were his arms. He must have hit the gravel at speed.

Dray nodded to Ed to get the water, but he was already handing Forest the skin. He pulled at the boot and the man called out, almost dropping the water skin. Ed frowned at him.

"We have a long way to go, and I need to be sure that we can make it."

"You would leave me behind?" Forest asked incredulously, trying to make it to his feet.

"Of course not. I just need to see what we are dealing with." The man's ankle was black with bruising and already swollen. It didn't appear to be broken, but Dray couldn't be sure. He wished they had someone who could help, someone who could magic it all away, but he knew they couldn't ask for such a thing. He pulled out a shirt from the bag. As Ed opened his mouth to protest, he tore a long strip from one side and then the other.

He manoeuvred the foot into position. As Forest cried out, Ed took his arm. They worked together to strap the foot and get it back in the boot. He needed to rest it, possibly for days, but they didn't have that long. They needed to make it to the forest, and the longer they took the less chance they had of reaching it. Ana knew exactly where they were. She had taken Belle and then their horses. It was only a matter of time before she stepped from the shadows and took one of them.

Ed fussed over the sword master as Dray moved with long strides back out to the road. They needed another option—they needed a chance. He walked a little further along the road and was sure he could see a farm in the distance. Or at least a cottage. And where there was one, there was likely to be another. He glanced over his shoulder and then took off at a fast jog towards the cottage. He banged on the door, but no one answered. A thin trail of smoke coiled its way up into the sky, and he knew they were hiding. He walked around the cottage and noticed another building across the yard. He headed for it and pushed the door open without knocking.

A boy rubbed at an old horse while it ate. He jumped with fear as Dray strode forward. Dray wished for his armour and a simpler time, when he could claim to be what he had once been.

"I need your horse," he said without preamble.

The boy shook his head. Dray looked into the other corner of the barn and then stepped forward.

"And the cart."

"It is all we have," the boy pleaded.

Dray rubbed at his too-long hair and then across his bearded chin. He wasn't the man he had been. He rested his hand on his sword, drawing the boy's attention. "I want to tell you that I will return it, that it is for a good cause. But I can't promise you anything. We have run out of options, and all I ask is that you help your king, or I take it." He didn't mean for the words to sound as harsh as they did, but he didn't have the luxury of kindness. The longer they took, the more likely they were to die.

"King?" the boy asked.

Dray nodded once, but the boy didn't move. "Come with me to see for yourself."

"The queen," the boy whispered, looking around the barn.

"She already knows where we are," Dray admitted. "Please," he tried.

The boy shook his head and raced out of the barn towards the house.

Dray cursed under his breath, looking from the horse to the cart. He hoped this could be done quickly. As it was, no matter that he wasn't family, the horse allowed him to hitch her to the cart quietly. He saw an old blanket across the edge of the stable and tossed it into the cart. It was small, but big enough for him and the king to ride at the front while Forest could sit in the back. He double-checked the reins, climbed up onto the cart and flicked to get the horse moving. It plodded along, and he glanced at the house as he passed, waiting for someone to challenge him. He thought he saw a face in the window and nodded his thanks, then flicked the reins harder. The horse moved into a trot, and he headed back to the king.

When he reached the space they had been, they were gone. "Ed!" he called into the trees in the chance they were hiding.

When Ed poked his head around a tree, Dray nodded slowly, trying not to sigh with relief. He was tired and just wanted this over. Ed stepped forward and looked at the cart.

"This looks like Phillip's."

"Well, if you have travelled this way before, you won't mind doing it again."

"Anything is better than walking." Ed disappeared behind the tree and helped Forest to limp out. The man scowled at the carriage. Dray climbed down and helped Ed lift him into the back.

"It is not going to be that comfortable, but it will give your ankle a chance. I fear we are going to need every man we can when we meet her."

"That could be on the way," Ed said. "I've been so focused on the trees. Do you really think she will let us reach them?"

"I don't know if she cares enough to stop us. It just seems to be game playing. But we will have to face her at some stage, and I fear that will be when she is willing, not when we are ready."

"And Belle?" Ed asked, climbing up into the front bench as Dray did the same from the opposite side.

"Let's just hope she is still headed in the same direction."

"You dreamt it," Ed said, raising his voice over the sound of the wheels on the road.

"Things can change," Dray said, his eyes forward. He was

starting to doubt they were headed in a direction they could win. Ana had too many eyes on them. She was too strong. They had thought they were moving to outsmart her, but no one could. She saw it all, understood it all, and she could change the balance in a moment by stealing a horse or removing a team member.

Belle hadn't visited him again. Dray didn't know if that was because of something the mage had done, or Ana, or Belle herself had thought better of it, or if she simply wasn't able to do it again. He still felt the same fear when she had walked into his dream, that she was another with skills he would never understand.

Although they had been counting on that. Trying to help her work out what she was and how her magic worked so she could help them stand against Ana. And so far, she hadn't worked it out. But if she did, Ana might remove her before she was a threat, like the little girl in the throne room. Dray felt sick.

He blinked into the light, took a deep breath and turned to Ed, a king sitting beside him with his hands on his arm. Dray raised an eyebrow, but the king didn't move.

"We are doing the right thing," Ed said.

"How can you be so certain?"

"Because you were," Ed said calmly. "You know what is best; you know her best."

Dray shook his head, and Ed smiled.

"I trust in you and your plan."

"And if that plan gets you killed?"

"I will haunt you for the rest of your days, which would likely not be many."

Dray smiled in return. "At least we'll go together."

The man in the back of the cart groaned. Dray glanced over his shoulder to ensure he was as comfortable as he could be. "Get this thing moving," he said, thumping the side of the cart. Dray flicked the reins, and the horse cantered along the track, the cart bouncing around beneath him as it hit every rock and every dip in the road.

❁

"Explain that again," Ana said, her tone dangerous, and the child bowed lower.

"They are moving."

"Who? Tell me, show me," she hissed, stepping down from the throne and putting her hand on the child's head. Too many faces swam through her vision and the lord, his hair greying at the edges, his features worried. "The Lord of the Grassland," Ana hissed.

"Where is he going?" a soldier asked, and Ana looked up as he stepped forward.

"Grant, this is not for you."

"Still waiting for my title," he said with a smile.

She growled, and he stepped back. "This is not for you," she hissed.

"I can help you, Majesty. Let me and my men prove ourselves. We can fight just as well."

She nodded once. He backed out of the room.

"Stupid men," the child hissed.

"They are useful. My aim is to rule over these men. And they try, constantly, to fight against me. The lord was loyal. What changed?"

"The son," the creature hissed.

"He came willingly. The other lord, from the desert?"

"She moves forward to meet the grasslands, although they will not meet until they are nearly at the forest. They think about a meeting, on how to serve you."

"They use our skills to trick us, perhaps. Or are you mistaken? Do they meet to see how the provinces can support me, what they can offer me?"

"You want to believe the men of this land have accepted you as their queen."

Her growl filled the room as she lashed out at the child before her, marking its face in her anger. "I am Queen."

It stood too long staring at her before bowing low and nudging forward with its head.

"I could destroy you," she hissed.

*The child knows you are Queen. It is correct, the people of this land do not appreciate us.*

"I am Queen," she said again and blinked from the room, appearing in the small space where the blonde girl stood by the window looking out over the world. "What is their plan?"

"Who?" Belle asked, turning from the window as though Ana had interrupted her at something.

Ana growled out her frustration and the room shook, but the girl did not even flinch. Ana scowled at her.

"There is nothing you could do to me," she said.

"I could kill Ed," Ana whispered.

"You could try," Belle said, looking back out the window.

"I will have respect. I know what I am. You are nothing, a girl with a skill you can't master. And they have left you behind. Tell me their plan and I may help you."

"You only help yourself," Belle said without turning from the window. "I don't know what the plan is. There probably is no plan. How can they win against you?"

"They are trying."

"Are you worried they will win?" Belle asked, turning and taking her in. Was that pity Belle felt for her? Ana blinked back to the throne room, where the child was gone. She had no idea where to go. She couldn't lose this—she wouldn't lose this. She needed to rethink.

Ed had no power. He had no one to back him. The people were loyal to her, whether through fear or otherwise, and she wanted to believe no one would stand up against her. But the doubt had been sown.

# 23

Salima banked, the air rushing over her scales and under her wings. It was cool but not cooling, and she smiled. Ende, on the other hand, flying close behind her, felt more concern than joy at their flight. Their proximity to the city would alert Ana, she knew. But Ana was preoccupied, and this was their best chance.

As they circled the castle, she could hear the screams and feel the fear of the people below. Although desperate to reach her target here, Salima knew that as soon as they touched their feet to the ground, the shadows would attempt to consume them. Or at least stop them. She wasn't sure how a shadow could consume a dragon, but she wasn't going to risk finding out.

She hadn't fully explained to Ende why they were in the capital, but he had sensed Belle first. She followed his lead and the curve of the wall before she saw the woman glowing bright in the window. Belle waved at them and then disappeared.

Hovering close to Ende while trying to ignore the fear of those beneath her, Salima breathed her flames onto the pale stone of the castle. The glass melted and ran away, and then Ende was doing the same. The stone buckled. He landed against the side of the building, pushing it in. For a moment, Salima feared for Belle, but she appeared soon enough, a broad smile on her lips. Then Salima could sense her fear as she turned to look behind her, where shadows filled the room. Without hesitating, she leapt forward over the fallen rocks and into the air.

Salima swooped down and caught her easily, although she was sure her heart was in her throat. That was some trust the woman had in her. Ende leapt from the building as the shadows moved out towards him, and then they were flying out across the city and the marshes and the water. Salima expected questions or the like from the woman she held tight against her chest, but there were none.

She followed Ende's lead as they flew north along the coast, out over the water rather than the land. Salima knew they had left Ed behind, but they continued north. When Ende banked, she followed him above the trees of the Near Forest. The canopy was dense, and she could sense the shadows around it, although not in as great a number as they could have been. Ende dove straight down. She was sure he would take out trees as he dropped, but she trusted him to know what he was doing. She followed, and it was almost as though the trees opened up for her. She landed softly in a small clearing, releasing Belle in the same movement.

As Salima changed into the girl Belle would know, Belle wrapped her arms around her and kissed her cheek. "Dray said you would come," she said, skipping over to Ende who beamed at her as she threw her arms around him as well.

"He is something special," Ende replied.

"Do you know what he is?" Belle asked.

"A soldier," Ende said, resting his hand on her shoulder as she stepped back. She shook her head as though she didn't quite believe him. "Ed?" he asked, looking across at Salima.

"Still coming." Salima closed her eyes. "They might need some help."

"Ana has been playing games," Belle said. "I don't think she ever thought us a threat, but something has changed."

Salima nodded. The end had begun. She just hoped she could help enough to make it end as she hoped it would.

"Are you going to get him?" Belle asked, looking between the two of them, but Ende shook his head.

"We need to meet with others and work on some things first.

Like you and your light."

Belle shook her head. "It isn't there."

"Of course it is," Salima said. "I can see it now."

Belle shook her head and walked towards the trees at the edge of the clearing. Salima doubted she was headed anywhere but away from the sense of uncertainty she felt. She couldn't see the light. As Salima watched, Belle turned slowly and looked back at her.

"You can make fire," she said.

"I don't think the forest is the best place to see that," a voice like the wind whispered across her skin. Belle turned towards the man standing by a tree, just where she had been headed to.

"Eilke," she said, bowing a little. "I wouldn't suggest they risk your forest. It is something someone said, that the fire of the dragons might burn away the shadows."

Salima turned to Ende, who watched the others with a small smile. "It hasn't been tested," she said.

"Could you show me?" Belle asked. "If I do have the light you think I do, maybe that will help. The mage thought so, only he didn't really believe in dragons."

"I think we should ask permission to stay before you start having us show you fire in a forest," Ende said, stepping forward and putting his hand on her shoulder. "We will talk with the Near Folk and then find Ed."

Belle nodded and turned back to Eilke, who disappeared between the trees. Salima followed along behind, but she thought more of Ed. He knew how to take care of himself and had Dray with him. But the world was changing, and their chances of survival with it.

The village that opened up before them took her breath away. Ende took her hand and dragged her forward when she stopped at the tree line. People stopped what they were doing and watched them walk by. Children running around stopped and bowed their heads when they saw her and Ende. The sky above them was open.

She could feel the heat of the sun, although it wasn't as it had been for them in the desert. She tried to stop and take it all in, but Ende pulled her forward while Belle and Eilke disappeared into the building at the end of the road.

"You don't mind the trees," she said to Ende.

"I found it hard the last time we were here, very confining. But the need is greater now, and you are here."

She gave his hand a squeeze and followed Belle into the building.

An older man sat at the end of a long table. Although the ceiling of the building showed the sky, Salima felt the confines of the space and just how hard this was for Ende.

"Welcome," the man said, indicating the table. "You are safe here. We offer our protection as best we can, but we too know what is coming."

"You will take in the king," Belle said, and he nodded. "Will you fight with him?"

"In our way," the man said, looking from her to Salima. "Child, you are welcome to use your flames to train the girl."

Salima wasn't quite sure what she could do to help Belle. She had thought Belle had discovered her own power by now. She nodded her head and then looked back towards the villagers standing silent, watching the building they were in.

"How can you keep the shadows at bay?" she asked.

"They have been here before," Belle said.

The man nodded at Belle and then turned back to Salima. "We know what they are, and the trees work now to keep them away. They will not penetrate here again."

"Ana helped with the last time," Belle said. "Could she not work out a way to help them in?"

"It is her magic that allows us to keep them out. She used our magic and infused her own through the trees. Shared what was hers. She is not what she was." He looked down, and Salima could feel the sadness within him at what had been lost with Ana. "But in many ways, she has helped us protect ourselves from her."

"What of the Lord of Near Forest?" Belle asked.

"He and his people are close. The forest looks after its own."

Belle opened her mouth to say something else and then closed it. Salima was sure she had heard those words before, but she wasn't sure how that could help them at this time.

Then her father was standing, and Salima followed his lead to find Eilke at the door already. They followed him through the village to a set of cottages away from the others with a clearing beside it, although the trees were still very close. He indicated the space with his head and then walked away.

"Tell me more about your magic," Salima said to Belle without waiting for Eilke to make it far.

"I don't think I have any. Everyone talks of a glow, a light, but I don't shine. I do feel things. I sense something, something in Dray, but I do not glow."

"What sort of something in Dray?" Ende asked. "There is nothing there."

"And yet he senses things, like Ana and magic. He knew what you were," Belle said to Salima. "He knew that you would return."

"Because I told him I would. But there is a link with Ana."

"It broke," Belle said hurriedly, "when she became Queen. It was like the link between them was severed. She didn't know where we were or what we were doing."

"There is always a link," Ende said, walking towards one of the cottages. "It was always there between them, and it always will be."

Belle watched after him as he disappeared inside the small cottage, then turned back to Salima. "I thought he didn't like small spaces."

"He is what he needs to be. I wonder at the link between Ana, Dray and Ed."

"I'm sure it is broken," Belle said again. "When will you go for him?"

"Soon," Salima said. "I would like you to show me what you can do."

Belle shook her head and looked at the ground. "I've had this fight with the mage," she said.

"Where is he?" Ende asked, reappearing from the cottage.

"Somewhere on the road between the capital and here. Ana put me with him for a time, and then they took me to that strange room in the castle."

"What did the mage want?"

"To use me," Belle huffed. "To see me shine. I can't be what you need me to be," she said, her voice catching in her throat. Salima felt the disappointment ebb from her.

"You already shine," she said kindly, stepping forward.

Belle shook her head. "I've tried, but I can't."

"Try again," Salima coaxed.

Belle shook her head and raced towards one of the cottages, then slammed the door after her. Salima sighed.

"Can she be of use?" Ende asked.

Salima shrugged. She didn't know how to help Belle or show her what she could be. If she couldn't see or sense the glow within, she wouldn't be able to strengthen it. "Did you see her shine?"

He shook his head.

"You've known her for a while," she prompted.

"She was with Ed when we met. But she is just a girl. She doesn't have anything I could sense."

"Your senses might be clouded."

"Clouded?" he asked, his voice louder than the small space required.

"You found something else that took your attention," Salima said with a grin.

He stepped forward and wrapped large, warm arms around her. "You see it," he whispered across her hair.

She nodded against him. She just didn't know how to make Belle see it.

# 24

Ana stood in the shadows and watched the procession move past her. There were far more men than she would have liked to see for a discussion on trade and tribute. The lord rode towards the front, his mind on crops and grasses. She could almost smell the sweet green growth as she focused on him. They weren't in a hurry, and yet they travelled at a dignified pace. She wondered as she watched him if he had slept or ridden through the night, for he didn't look like a man who had slept much of late.

His mind turned to his missing son, cursing his stupidity and impulsive nature. Always running. He turned to a man beside him. "Any sign of the boy?"

"I am sorry, my lord, but he appears to have made it further away than he usually does. I'm sure he will be at the castle when we return from the talks."

The lord nodded, but she felt his doubt. Perhaps he needed a new bride, a new chance at a family. He thought the boy had run near their homeland. He had before. If the boy suddenly appeared at the forest, he might be suspicious. This lord was brighter than most she had come across. He was level and thought things through. Unlike the Lord of Near Forest, who was impulsive and young and constantly angry. He just wanted power, and he didn't care how he got it.

Ana's aunt had been something very different again. But then, she too had done what she could to hold on to power that hadn't belonged to her. Ana blinked away from the slow procession to a place she had once known so well. The cold grey walls were almost a comfort, as was the breeze blowing through the opening in the wall.

"You will come if you are called," she told the woman at the desk. She would do what Ana needed of her, although she should have left her to do as she was directed.

"They do not know, Majesty. They are too stupid to work it out."

There was a single knock at the door, and Ana stepped back into the shadows as a child appeared with a tray. The woman at the desk waved at the table across the room without looking up as Ana drank in the child's fear. She put the tray down with a shaky hand and curtsied, although too shallow in Ana's opinion, then disappeared back through the door, which she closed too loudly behind her.

The woman at the desk raised her eyebrows at Ana.

She stepped forward with a smile. "You are Lord," she said. "And if I need your soldiers, you will bring them."

"Majesty," the child said, standing from behind the desk and bowing low.

She blinked back to the throne room, waiting to be chastised for leaving it again, and found Grant striding into the room.

"Majesty," he said, bowing low. "I have been looking for you."

"Really?" she asked as several children appeared in the room, and he staggered back.

"Majesty, dragons have taken the girl."

She glared at the soldier. "How did they know where she was?"

Silence filled the room. Ana blinked to the small, enclosed space she had placed Belle. The wall was buckled, the windows melted. Stone lay across the floor and, when she leaned out of the opening, across the ground beneath.

"When?" she hissed.

"Hours ago, Majesty."

"Hours!" she screamed, more rocks tumbling from the damaged wall. "Why did you not come to me directly?"

"We could not." The child hung its head.

Ana waited, her anger burning inside her. She wanted to rip every one of them to a shadowy mess.

"The dragon's fire was white hot and bright and…" the child closest to her almost whimpered. Ana turned then and took him in properly, placing a hand on his arm, feeling the same burning pain.

"It was too bright," another hissed.

"You were hurt," she whispered.

The creatures nodded. "It took too long to heal."

"But you did," Ana said. "They are not that strong, only enough to slow us down. But with our numbers, that won't be possible."

"Majesty?" a child hissed.

"Prepare the soldiers; prepare the children. We are taking this fight to the boy, and we will end it. I will not have my family attacked."

They bowed to her and disappeared into the shadows of the room.

*We were wrong to think them not a threat.*

"And we will rectify that." Ana looked out over the city from the ruined wall of the room. Perhaps the people would fight against a king who used dragons.

Dray flicked the reins again, and Ed was thrown back in the seat. "What are you doing?" he asked, looking back at the semiconscious man being tossed around in the back.

"I want to get out of the trees."

"Why?"

"Something is coming. And I don't think we want to be under cover when it comes."

"Is Belle right about you?" Ed asked, the wind blowing through his hair. He was fighting to stay on the seat, but Dray wasn't slowing.

Dray glanced at Ed, gave a little shrug and flicked the reins again.

"We are going to lose Forest." Ed reached over the seat, trying to somehow hang on while hold the man's clothes so he didn't bounce out of the cart. And then they were in the open, through the small area of trees, and he could see just what was coming. Two dragons flew towards them. He could almost hear the sound of the air moving around their wings. It was a small amount of hope he hadn't had for far too long.

And they weren't slowing. Dray continued forward at his unsafe speed, and Ed was sure they would all fall to their deaths. Then Salima and Ende were flying over them. He looked up as they went by, then turned as too many shadows suddenly appeared out of the trees. Despite the creatures racing towards them, Dray pulled the horse to a stop and jumped down.

"What are you doing?" Ed asked, drawing his sword. But as he made to follow, Dray held up a hand.

"Stay where you are," he said, cutting the horse free. It raced off into the distance much faster than Ed thought it capable. The cart had started to tip forward, but Dray held it up. Forest groaned something behind him. Feeling the heat of fire, Ed chanced a glance to see the trees behind them alight, the shadows gone. Dray grunted, holding on to the cart. Then something large blocked out the sun above him.

Ed swallowed as a dragon hovered over the cart, closing large taloned claws around the edge of it. As it started to lift into the air, Dray scrambled back into the seat, a wide grin on his face. Ed squeezed his eyes closed as they moved around and grabbed tightly to his seat.

It felt like only moments and a lifetime at the same time before the cart touched down and pitched slowly forward. Ed opened his eyes to see Belle standing in the forest, tears streaming down her cheeks, and then she ran towards him.

He jumped down and scooped her up, spinning her around.

"I see you found your light," Dray said, helping Ende lift Forest from the back of the cart as Salima held up the other end. Ed looked at her for a moment; she appeared like the girl he knew and yet not. He turned back to Belle as she shook her head and buried it back in Ed's chest.

"She can't see it," Salima said, lowering the cart as they half carried the man towards one of the cottages.

"You'll need to find it soon," Dray called over his shoulder. "Looks like light is the only way to slow them down."

Belle looked up at Ed, and he shook his head.

Salima wrapped her arms around them both. "It appears that you were right," she said to Belle. "The dragon fire certainly did some damage. But it doesn't kill them."

"Could it be enough that a sword would then work?" Ed asked.

Salima shook her head. "I don't know," she said. "It is good to see you, but I need to check on Papa."

"He came off a horse, hard."

She was already walking away, but she nodded as she went. Not long after, Eilke walked through the small clearing and into the cottage. Then another Near Folk followed and Ende was pushing his way out, shaking his head.

"Too tight?" Ed asked, now sitting in the grass with his arm around Belle.

The dragon smiled, and Ed realised he had missed that mysteriously perfect grin. It had been too long since they had been together. But even with them all together now, he wasn't sure it would be enough.

"Where were you?" he asked Belle.

"With the mage, and then at the castle."

"The castle?"

"Something happened, something changed, and she pulled me

there to answer her questions. Please tell me I will never be dragged through the shadows again."

"Not as long as I can stop it," Ed reassured her, pulling her closer. But he wasn't sure he would ever be able to stop them doing just what they wanted. Particularly Ana. "What changed?"

"I don't know, but she wanted to know your plans."

"We never really had any. And any we did haven't been of use." He looked up at the dragon watching them. "But having a dragon or two certainly helps."

"Let's hope so," Ende murmured as Eilke came out of the cottage.

"Not as bad as it looked. He needs rest and food."

"Thank you," Ed said, climbing to his feet and holding out his hand to the man. Eilke took him by the forearm and shook it firmly.

"We will help all we can, Your Majesty, but we will not leave the trees."

Ed opened and closed his mouth, then gave the Near man a nod. For now, it would be enough that they were safe in the trees. He only hoped they had enough time to work out how they could end this without the Near Folk.

# 25

Ana cried out as the children slowly appeared around her. Grant stood to the side, his face unreadable, but fear and uncertainty were radiating from him. As they radiated from the children as they appeared.

"What has taken so long?" she asked. But she knew the answer. The dragons.

"The fire burns," one child hissed, dropping to his knees before her. "They cannot kill us, but it takes longer than we would like to come back from the damage. The light is so bright."

Ana growled, the sound filling the space around her.

*We can no longer wait for them. We must destroy them now.*

"How do we destroy a dragon?" she murmured, then looked up as Grant made his way slowly towards the door. "You will not run," she said, raising her hand to him, and he stopped. "You will gather your men, every man you can trust and those you hope you can. Prepare, for we will take this fight to them."

"Majesty." He bowed his head but remained unmoving. She flicked her hand, and ran for the door.

"We do not need them," one child hissed.

"We need them more than I would like. They cannot kill us. But slowing us down might be more than enough to save their king. The more we have, the more we can outrun the dragons. There are only two of them and so many more of us. How long did it take you to recover?"

"It depends how close they are, how much flame we feel."

Ana nodded slowly. This was something they could work around. They might think that they had force, but she wouldn't be beaten.

Ana stood on the balcony and looked over the city before her. It felt as it always had, and yet she felt nervous for the first time in too long. She was Queen; she had power. And she had known that the dragons would be a problem. But they had left the king to her and disappeared far from the action. She had been too dismissive of their power.

Salima, the little dragon, had always been too focused on her brother. She would be behind this. Ende would have quietly disappeared into obscurity, or his mountains. Ana slammed her fist down on the balustrade, cracking the stone.

*They cannot kill us.*

"It is not enough," she whispered. "They can harm us, harm the children."

*Two against so many.*

And Ana would make sure there were more. They would stay close to those they knew; Salima would remain close to her brother. Ende, she wasn't as sure of. They only had a small force— Ana had the kingdom behind her.

She blinked into the throne room and sat heavily in the cold stone throne as Grant stood before it, staring.

"What do think you can do against me?" she asked.

"I support you, Majesty, at every step. The men are ready." He looked up, staring for a moment eye to eye as though she were nothing to fear. "I will follow wherever you lead." He bowed his head, and she sighed. He was useful for now, but she wondered what he would expect if he survived this.

*Ensure he doesn't.*

Ana nodded her head once. "Horses, carriages, whatever you need. Your task is to get your men as close to the Near Forest as possible, as soon as possible."

"And you, Majesty?"

She stood slowly, feeling the stone crack beneath her hands as she used the armrests to push herself up. "I will be waiting when you get there."

He bowed low. A flash of fear gave Ana the strength she needed, and he was racing from the room.

*They will be enough.*

"I hope so," she said, sitting slowly back on her throne, the crown still heavy on her head. A child appeared before her. "Where are the lords?"

"Not close enough," he hissed, bowing before her.

"They will reach the battleground too late," she whispered. "If it isn't already."

"When, Majesty?"

"Give the men time to get there, and we will follow."

"We do not need them," he hissed. "We are strong enough to destroy the boy."

Ana nodded. "But they will fight with us. And the mage?"

"Walking slowly."

She laughed. He was never of any use. She would deal with him too when this was all over.

Dray watched the girl struggle in the clearing. She didn't believe in herself. He knew it, he sensed it, and yet he didn't want to tell her what she already knew. It would only draw her attention back to him. Not that he was what she thought he might be. He was a soldier; he just saw more than most.

Despite the look of concentration on her face, Belle shone a little brighter than she had before. Dray wondered if that was what he saw or what he wanted to see. He turned to the dragon beside him.

"She is something," Ende said, but as Dray looked back he wasn't sure if he meant the girl or the dragon.

"She is stronger than you," Dray said, thinking of the dragon. Ende nodded. "Has she told you what she has seen?"

Ende shook his head, still watching them, but he said nothing. Dray wondered just how much he did see. Salima stopped and stood rigid for a moment before turning around to them. Dray's stomach dropped, sure she had seen something more that he did not want to hear.

"She is coming," she whispered, and yet the sound travelled across the whole forest.

Ed came out of the cottage, Forest not far behind. But before anything else could be said, Eilke appeared from the trees and motioned Dray forward.

"There is a man you should see," he said, turning and walking into the trees.

Dray left the group behind him with barely a glance. There was nothing they could do to change what was coming; they just had to be prepared to face it.

He walked out of the trees into a makeshift camp, although it looked more permanent than temporary. The Lord of Near Forest walked towards him, and then he saw the shine of King's Men armour and drew his sword.

"That is no way to treat an old friend," Barlow said. Dray sheathed his sword as the man walked fast towards him, took his arm and shook it, slapping him on the shoulder.

"It is good to see you," Dray said, trying hard to hide his smile.

"Where did you come from?" the lord asked. Dray turned his attention to him, bowed his head and vaguely pointed over his shoulder.

"Another comes," Eilke said, disappearing again into the trees.

"The witch?" the lord asked.

Dray shook his head. "She is not far away, but she can't make it through the trees."

"Are we sure?" the man asked.

Dray nodded. "But we will have to face her. Can the king count on your support?"

"The king is here?" Barlow asked.

"With the Near Folk, and Master Forest and…" He wasn't quite sure how he could tell them what allies they had.

"Tell me you have a way," Barlow implored.

"We think we do," Dray said. "But we will need more men to assist us." He turned again to the lord, who looked over the people around the camp and then nodded, although he didn't turn back to Dray.

"We will never be free while she is Queen," he whispered.

"The shadows are too strong," one of Barlow's men said, joining them.

"We have a way to weaken them, but it is limited. I don't know how effective we can be. It might be that we can slow her down while we make a run for the capital. But I hope we can end this once and for all."

"How?" the man asked.

Dray looked at Barlow and grinned.

"You found the dragon," he said.

"A dragon?" another voice asked, and Dray drew his sword a second time as the mage walked towards him.

"How?" Dray asked.

"I have more magic than you would think. The girl may never work it out, but one dragon might not be enough either."

"What about two?" Dray asked. The old man staggered back and sat heavily in the grass.

"Two dragons," Barlow said slowly. "Will they be enough against a whole army of shadow monsters? And I'm sure there are some in the King's Men who would fight with her."

"We might have more, and the dragons can hit many shadows at once. It will be up to us to follow."

"You have my support and those who are willing to follow," the lord said.

"The Lord of the Grassland and Lord of the Dry will come," Salima said, walking out from the trees. She looked at the mage still sitting in the grass and growled at him, making the forest shake around them.

"You can eat him later," Dray whispered, not very quietly. "Are you sure about the lords?" He knew she was, and she gave him a look that reflected just that.

"If she has left with her men as well as her shadows, it might be that men loyal to the king will follow," Barlow offered.

"Will she bring her full force?" the lord asked.

"To face a dragon, yes, it is the only way," Dray said.

"They seem stronger now she is Queen," Barlow said.

"Not strong enough," Salima said. "The king would like to talk with you," she said to the lord. "Are you happy if I send him out?"

"Send the king?" Barlow stammered. "You are just the daughter of a soldier."

"She is far more than that," Dray said, leaning in close to the man, "and the king will listen."

He bowed his head to her, and she smiled as she turned and disappeared back between the trees. She appeared to do as any princess would to support her king. She was far more comfortable in the forest than Ende had been, but then she saw more.

# 26

Ed joined the lord by the fire as the night set in around them. The shadows made him look in case there was something else out there, something else coming. He had to remind himself that they were safe within the trees.

"I am sorry, Your Majesty," the lord said, although his attention was on the people around him. "I didn't fully appreciate who you were and what you could do for the kingdom."

Ed said nothing. There was nothing he could say. None of them could have predicted how this had gone, except maybe Ende. He looked back towards the trees that led to the Near Folk village, where Salima was still trying to help Belle find something she was sure she didn't have.

"We are grateful for your support," Dray said. His voice was low, but it carried through the clearing and several people looked up at him.

"The king was lucky you stayed with him," Barlow said.

Ed wasn't really sure that Dray had the choice. Ana had turned on him in just the same way. But he was grateful the man had remained close, or he might have been lost several times over.

"I knew you would do what you could," Ed said to the other soldier.

"It wasn't easy," Barlow murmured, looking back at the men standing to the edge of the main camp. "She sees so much."

"Will the dragons be enough?" the lord asked, turning to Ed.

Ed nodded slowly. "I hope so," he said, and the man raised his eyebrows in surprise. "It certainly weakens them, but it is so hard to kill a shadow. Perhaps in their weakened state we can finish off the men inside them, but it is an idea only."

"I suppose there is no way to test it until we are in the fight."

Ed looked down. He realised he was asking far more of these people than he deserved. They had hoped the increased numbers would be enough. But there were no guarantees, and it might not be that easy. The shadow monsters were so much stronger. They could steal them or consume them rather than fight, and this might all be over before they had a chance to leave the trees.

Ed cleared his throat as Dray laid a hand on his shoulder. He meant for the action to show support, and Ed felt that, but he also felt the weight of the kingdom behind that hand. He wasn't sure it would be possible to win this, and there was far more to lose if they lost. Ana would make them all pay for angering her.

He looked back towards the clearing and wondered if the damage the dragons had done was what pushed her. Although she didn't seem as interested or threatened by them, he knew she would tire of playing with them at some stage and want them removed from the game altogether.

"Who will lead us out from the trees?" the lord asked.

"The dragons will start. They will be safely out of reach and can cause as much damage as possible to the shadow monsters. Then we move."

The lord nodded and turned back to his men.

"I know this is a lot to ask," Ed said, but the man held up a hand.

"It is what any king would expect of his people, and this is our land too. We fight with you."

Ed bowed his head to the lord in gratitude. Then he turned his attention to Barlow. "Do you think there will be men amongst the soldiers who would stand with us?"

"Yes," Barlow said simply, "but we may not know who they are until the fighting starts. Any man who had a single thought against her has been consumed or sent away."

"Sent away?" Dray asked.

"Beyond," Barlow said.

Ed looked at Dray and then back to the soldier. "You mean she killed them."

"Most likely, but she claimed to have sent them to learn."

Ed dragged in a deep breath and turned back to Dray. He might have accepted that the Ana he had known was gone, but there was still a sense of disappointment and loss on the large man's face.

"I might see how the little light is going," Dray murmured, walking slowly away. The mage stepped into the light of the fire and opened his mouth to say something, but Ed shook his head and glared at him.

He didn't trust this man at all. Anything he did suggest was most likely to benefit him rather than anyone else in the kingdom.

"She might respond to him," the mage said quickly.

The lord turned and looked him over as though trying to consider the best way to reply.

"There is no link between them," Ed said.

"There is always a link," the mage murmured, but the grin he wore diffused any chance of Ed believing him.

"The witch will not fall for a trick; she cares for no one but herself," Barlow growled, and the old man shrugged and stepped back.

Ed was reminded of the shadow creatures, but the Near Folk had assured him they couldn't find their way into the forest. He wondered who else the mage might whisper his crazy plans to.

The Near Folk had promised to follow Ed. Although they wouldn't leave the trees, the Lord of Near Forest was clearly unsure of the world beyond. He had no idea how close the other lords might be.

Particularly when Ana could arrive at any time. It wasn't just fighting the shadow creatures—it was Ana as well. They would have to face her at some point, and they would need to find a way to defeat her. That was the reason behind Dray's sadness, Ed was sure. Not just that it had come to this, but that he knew they would have to kill her.

The idea both terrified him and made him very sad. She was no longer the woman he had met in the mountains, and that was the very reason they were here. But she was so much stronger; she could move so much further. She might be back in the castle in a heartbeat before a sword could even be raised against her.

"Thank you," Ed murmured to the lord and headed back for the trees. He couldn't dwell on such a thing or the whole group would give up and allow her to win. As he entered the small clearing around the cottages they had been provided, he stopped, taking in the glowing woman before him.

"Belle," he called. She looked up at him, fading slightly, and then the light went out.

"I can't do it," she said, dropping to the ground.

"You were doing it," he said.

"You saw me glow?"

He nodded and looked around the clearing to find Salima standing a short distance away. She nodded slowly and then walked away.

"Everyone can see it but me," Belle cried. "I will never learn to shine bright enough to do any damage, and I won't be able to direct it." She sighed and leaned into him as he sat beside her in the dark. "I am no use to you."

"You will shine," he reassured her.

"In time for a fight we can't win?"

He didn't know what he could say to that, so he just pulled her close and rested his cheek on her head.

"Ed?"

"Mmm."

"What are we going to do? How long have we got?"

"Not long," he murmured. "I expect she will push them through the night and they will arrive tomorrow evening."

"We'll be fighting them in the dark?" She sounded as scared as Ed felt, and he tried to keep his voice level when he answered her.

"I don't know."

Dray stood on the edge of the trees with Eilke and watched the distant dark clouds roll in. They were not far away; he could sense it, although he wasn't willing to say that to anyone. Belle might be struggling to work out what she was and how to use that skill, but she would take the chance to tease him if she could. Despite the fear surrounding what they were experiencing.

He had not slept well the night before, although he doubted anyone had. He had spent much of the night pacing the small clearing around the cottages. He had hoped to sleep a little, but it had refused to take him when he had lain down. He had fought before and wondered if he had a chance to win, yet this felt so very different. Their chances were even smaller than he could hope for. They had based their whole plan on the idea that the dragons would be enough, and he knew they weren't.

There was more to this than light. They were fighting creatures created from another world, led by a woman they could never best. He had wanted to voice that concern with someone, anyone. He had found Ende in the night, but he couldn't do it. Although he was sure the dragon had a good idea of what they were facing. Far better than Dray did, he imagined. It wasn't going to be enough to face these creatures—they would have to face Ana, and he didn't think he could do that. She might not be the girl he knew anymore, but he wouldn't be able to raise a sword to her.

He looked out at the coming storm and wondered if he would change his mind in the thick of battle, when he was fighting for more than his life. For a king, and a kingdom and all its people.

"Do you think the others are far?" he asked, wondering if the other lords and their men had managed to survive the journey north.

"We may not know."

Dray nodded once and turned from the tree line. There was nothing they could do now but prepare as best they could. As he walked back through the clearing on his way through to ensure the lord and his men were ready, he saw Belle glowing, her face twisted in concentration. He changed course.

"I can't do this," she whispered as he drew closer.

"You are doing it." He waved Salima over as she talked with Ende. He had noticed they spent a lot of time together, but they were family. And they needed to ensure they knew what they were doing.

"Dray." She gave him a bow of her head.

"Princess," he greeted, and she smiled in return. "Can you show Belle your light?"

"We are something very different," Salima said, her eyebrows drawn together.

"Just a little."

"What are you up to?" Belle asked.

"Watch," he instructed as Salima transformed before his eyes and breathed a small trail of fire. The flame was white hot. He wondered at how she had learnt such control.

"I am the fire," she said, looking at Belle.

"And you are the light," Dray said to her. "Focus on the feeling when she makes the flames."

"You don't know what you are doing," she returned. "You are always telling me you are a soldier and nothing special. How can you understand this?"

He shrugged. He wasn't sure he could explain it. He waved for Salima to do it again. And Belle watched the flames trace out and around.

"Do you have to be a dragon?" Belle asked.

"I am a dragon," Salima said, changing back into a girl. "I can make flames as a girl, but not with the same strength or heat. They are hot enough to burn, but not the same."

Belle closed her eyes and held her hands out before her, then opened her eyes as her hands began to glow. A small smile spread across her face, and the light increased.

"You can see it," he said.

She nodded and glowed a little brighter, but it wasn't enough. It wasn't going to be enough to do any damage to the shadows. Yet he didn't want to discourage her.

"Can you direct it?" Salima asked, glancing between the two of them.

Belle pointed towards Dray, but nothing changed. She squinted with concentration and tried again. Letting out a sigh, she dropped her hands to her sides.

"It is something," he said.

"I won't be able to master what I need before they come. How soon?" she asked.

Dray cleared his throat. "Soon," he said. "I need to talk to the king."

"Ende!" Salima called. "We need to slow them down." She took to the air, Ende not far behind.

Dray rested his hand on Belle's shoulders as she sighed. "You will find it," he whispered, and then he was running out through the trees in search of the king.

# 27

Ana cursed the voice inside her. She had trusted too long in the strength she thought she had. Knew she had. Yet these people, these insignificant people, had still managed to pull together more than she had ever expected them to. She watched the dragons soar distantly overhead like birds on the breeze, and yet they had forced most of her children into hiding.

She would win this. She had more power, more strength, than any of them anticipated.

*They cannot kill a shadow.*

"But they try," she murmured, watching the distant shapes and knowing they would come closer, knowing they were trying to distract her from the prize hiding inside the forest. This was her kingdom, and she wasn't going to give it up. The people followed her. They bowed down to her. Their soldiers fought for her.

They lined up in neat black rows moving towards the trees. She could feel their uncertainty at the shapes overhead, but she had assured them the dragons were only interested in the shadows. Their king expected them to turn and join him the moment they laid eyes on him. But they would never follow such a man.

She had waited all day, and they were yet to show their faces or their strength, if they had any, from within the trees. Again she cursed the magic in the trees. She had experienced it once, but she couldn't quite grasp it. Couldn't quite determine what it was so she could defeat it.

She looked to Grant who, appeared to sense her gaze, turned and nodded once. The men would have no trouble entering the trees. He took a line and marched forward. They would drive them out, push him out to meet her.

*You should never have let them go*, the voice within hissed cruelly. *If you had done as I wanted, we wouldn't be here.*

"You never offer anything of assistance. They will die now at my hand, and that is all we need consider," Ana said.

*You can't even reach them,* the voice mocked.

"Grant," Ana called, and he surged forward.

In the same instant, two things happened—soldiers raced from the trees, and a large dragon swooped down over her army. Ana looked up in awe. He was so much larger than she had imagined, than she had remembered. It appeared that more had joined the king but it didn't matter, it wouldn't be enough.

Ende spewed forth hot, white flames over the shadows below, they screamed out. They faded in and out of the sunshine and then disappeared. It was hard to kill a shadow, and Ana smiled at the chaos. They would repair and return. She breathed in the fear of the men running towards the trees and those running from them. Using it, she pulled more shadows from the world around them. They had no real form, but she could use them to steal the others or strengthen her own if needed.

The dragon flew over again, white-hot flames dissipating the shadows she had just pulled forward.

She screamed out in anger.

*Destroy him!* the voice inside her hissed.

Ana released her frustrations on the beast, but the smaller dragon aimed white flames at her and it took all she had to avoid them. Ende circled around, debilitating more of her children, and she screamed again.

Ana watched as her children faded. As some started to reappear amongst the lines of soldiers moving forward to meet the men coming from the trees, she closed her eyes and breathed in the chaos and fear around her.

As Ende circled around again, Ana reached towards him, following his path. When his mouth opened, Ana channelled the fear she had absorbed from those around her. The energy wrapped around him and he glowed hot, his wings faltering. His own fire consuming him from inside. He fell, dropping like a stone from the sky and crashing into the forest.

The world dropped to silence around her as she let out a slow breath. The only sound was the trees screaming. She breathed it in, replenishing her loss. She was stronger than she had ever been. Her own men at the ready, those at the tree line disappeared as the shadows grew around her. The world lost its sharp focus, and for a moment she was sure she was in the beyond as a thick mist formed around her. The sky darkened, and then a soldier was before her on bended knee in the mud.

"Majesty," he said, more awe than fear. Ana was a little disappointed. "What would you have us do?"

"Push them out. They will be in turmoil now. Go. Drive them from the trees."

He nodded once and raced away to join the men towards the tree line.

Ed stared at the giant fallen dragon before him. He'd had some idea that as a dragon Ende would be huge, but he'd had no idea he could be anything this large. The trees had snapped as he had fallen, some of them opening more wounds, but he was already gone. Whatever Ana had done to him had burned him from the inside out. Half of his face was blackened by his own flames, as was most of his body. His wings lay limp across the ground.

Salima stood silently beside him, as did the rest of those who had gathered to see if he could be saved. Ed reached out and took her hand. She flinched, then squeezed it back as though she hadn't realised he was there.

She blew out a small breath and then raised her eyes from the dragon she had only recently learnt was her father. Something angry seemed to set in her eyes. Ed's hand became warmer and warmer, and he pulled away from her.

"We must go out there," she whispered, but her voice carried like a rumble through the trees. "We must fight on, for she will not stop."

"I'm sorry," Ed murmured.

"I knew it was to come," Salima said, looking at him for the first time, her smile sad. "But that doesn't make it any easier."

He shook his head.

"The fire weakened them," Dray said. "I saw it. The shadows disappeared, although they came back. If we can use it on her shadow soldiers, we might have a chance."

Salima nodded, but the waiting soldiers and Near Folk remained silent.

"They will find a way into the trees," Belle murmured. A large tear tracked down her cheek as she stood by Dray, looking at the fallen dragon. "Salima is right. We must fight on or we will all be lost."

"She took down a dragon," someone called from the group. "We are all lost."

"Maybe," Ed murmured, then took in his sister's face. She seemed so much taller, so much older than he remembered her being. Had they been separated for so long? She gave him a sad smile. "But I cannot leave the kingdom to this woman. This witch," he said, trying not to turn and see what Dray might do to him. "We have a small chance, and if you don't believe it is worth the risk, you may remain in the trees or attempt to make it back to where you came from."

The other lords had joined them, only small numbers of soldiers behind them, but they bowed their heads to him. There was some murmuring amongst the other soldiers, but the majority of those present put their fists to their hearts and bowed low, following Dray's lead. Ed choked back the sudden overwhelming relief and nodded. He drew his sword, bowed his head to the fallen dragon, sucked in a deep breath and headed towards the tree line. It wouldn't be long before she was sending in the men after them.

"We might have to fight our own," he said.

"They are not our own if they fight with her," Barlow said, giving a nod to his men, and they moved out ahead of Ed.

As Ed looked to Dray, he could already hear sword on sword. He followed in their wake, where the queen's men had been pushed back or killed. Ed recognised faces amongst the few dead he could see. Dray paused by a man, and Ed stopped.

"I'm sorry," he said.

"How would you feel, Your Majesty, if I were to don my armour once more?"

"Relieved," Ed said honestly. And he gave the man a nod as he left him to take back what was his.

He paused in the tree line, watching the men rush away. Then, with the shadows moving around them, they stood their ground.

"I don't want you in this," Ed said to Belle, suddenly pulling her close. She grinned up at him, kissed him quickly and then started to shine. He knew she had the ability, and yet she had struggled; he wanted to be sure she could protect herself. "You are beautiful," he murmured.

"You are not leaving my sight," she said, and the shadows receded as they moved slowly from the trees.

Belle took a shaky breath. Ed wanted desperately to send her somewhere safe, but as he watched the shadows around them cringe away, he realised she was shining brighter.

"How?" he asked.

She shook her head, and the creatures around them cried out. As they did, Barlow stuck his sword in the nearest one. It didn't even fight back as a man crumpled to the ground and a shadow was lost to the mist surrounding them. It didn't matter how she'd found it. She had. They moved forward together, Belle shining while Ed and the small group around him destroyed any creature close enough.

# 28

The mist closed in around Dray, and he struggled to focus. The darkness seemed to make it harder and harder to know what he was fighting against. The steady sound of metal against metal, was punctuated with blood curdling screams. Then there was a flash of light and a groan, which Dray had quickly learnt meant a shadow was harmed enough that he could do some damage with a sword. It worked for men as well. There were far more of those in the King's Men armour, or a strange dulled version of it, who appeared to have the same shadow strengths, and Dray wondered what she had promised them.

A soldier loomed out of the mist before him, and he pushed forward with his sword to be met with a defensive blow. He only hoped that Belle or Salima was close and could do some damage soon. He tried again, the man far stronger than he'd expected. He might have recognised him from the barracks, but Dray had stopped looking at their faces. He was watching their bodies, trying to see signs that they weren't as human as they had been before.

Some soldiers had attacked him with strength, but they lacked fluidity. And once they were damaged by the light, it was enough to distract and weaken them so he could finish them off. The man before him was something different. He had the strength, but he moved like any good soldier Dray might have had within his command. He was fluid, masterful even, and Dray wondered if he might have trained with Forest.

Dray staggered back as a sharp blade across his face caught him by surprise. He wiped at the sting, too aware of the blood on his fingers, but trying not to look. The man grinned at him and licked his lips with a long dark tongue.

This was something else, some new creature that had infiltrated the fight. If there were more like him, Dray might never be able to determine who was what. But there was something about him, something familiar, and Dray knew he had met him. He might be a creature, but he still presented as a man. As the thought entered his head, the smile grew wider and wider on the other man's face. With the sword still gripped firmly in his hand, he changed before Dray's eyes into one of the very creatures he hoped to destroy.

It towered over him. But Dray had a strength too, and he had been fighting since he was a boy. He aimed low before the creature had a chance to fully change. The blow did little damage, although it managed to throw the creature off balance and it staggered backwards.

Screaming and shouting surrounded him, and he heard the whoosh of flames as the fog lit up around him. The creature before him grinned, then cried out as the flames touched its grey skin. Dray drove his sword through its chest before it had the chance to recover.

What had once been a man slumped to the ground before him as the shadow disappeared into the mist, making it darker and thicker. Dray looked around him. The whole world was dark. He wasn't sure if they were winning or making the other side stronger. Another flash of light, another scream, and he turned at the sound behind him, lifting his sword just as the creature was about to sink its thick claws into his back. He sliced in an upward motion, taking its fingers, and it screamed as it disappeared back into the mist.

To his right, he could see a steady glow, the mist not as thick around it. He headed in that direction, hoping it was Belle and the king. They were safer together. There were many fighting, but as the mist became thicker it was harder and harder to see who was nearby. Dray was starting to think he was fighting this all on his own.

He stopped at the sound of flames sizzling through the fog, and the white light burned away the mist before him. He saw the men near the king all fighting to keep him safe, Belle glowing brightly and the shadows held back.

In trying to reach them, Dray had to work his way through several others, men he knew—men he had once trusted with more than his life. All the while, his focus was on reaching the king. There was no sign of Ana amongst the blood and mud and mist. But then, he had to remind himself that she was gone. The witch behind all of this was likely orchestrating it from some safe distance.

A shadow monster appeared before him. Dray moved swiftly with his sword, but it passed right through the creature. And he was pushed by strong hands. Dray staggered back, trying not to lose his footing in the mud. His face stung, he was exhausted and there seemed no end to these creatures. It was as though she created more from those they managed to destroy. Dray wondered if he too would end up as one of them.

He had lost sight of the king and Belle, and the mist closed in around him. He struggled to remain focused, swinging again at the creature bearing down on him and making no impact.

The mage appeared from the mist beside him, his hand out and his eyes closed, and the creature appeared to slow. Dray pushed forward, determined to beat it, and although it had nowhere to go, he made no mark. Then the bright white light of dragon fire lit up the world around him and flashed over the creature. Its face changed in an instant, becoming Kemp. Dray drove his sword forward without hesitation, the flames catching his arm.

He bit back a cry, watching the man before him crumple and the mist darken again. The mage disappeared, and Dray wondered at the help from the man. What did he expect to get from the king by working with him?

More flames flared around him as Dray felt the fight in him fading. His sword dropped to his side. Too many creatures surrounded them. There were less soldiers now to protect the king. Ed's shiny sword flashed through grey skin in the light of Belle's glow. But he knew it wasn't enough.

Dray searched the surroundings for a chance, a small hope that they could end this, and he locked eyes with the woman in the mist. Her dark hair seemed to move on its own, her dress untouched by the horror of the field, although the hem was muddy. It was the look of fear on her face that made his heart stop and his face sting all the more.

Ana.

For a single moment, the witch queen—the woman trying to destroy the entire world, to bend it to her will and prevent a boy from taking what was his—stood amidst the carnage, the mist closing in around them, and she looked afraid.

Her green eyes were locked on his as he sheathed his bloody sword and strode towards her. It was time. No matter what she had been or what she could be, this had to end, and he might be the only one who could do that.

As he reached her, a single tear rolled down her cheek, her green eyes glowed brighter and her fingers reached for his face. Through the mist surrounding them, Belle stepped forward, her blonde hair glowing in the dim light although no sun had penetrated it. The scales of the dragon were reflected on the other side.

Dray nodded once and stepped up to the woman he still thought of every night, or at least mourned for. For this woman was not her, and yet here he was risking it all for her again. Only this time, he would die. This would be the last time he could try to save her, and he was certain to fail.

Something hardened in the woman before him, as though she realised in that moment that she wasn't what she had been. Her eyes glowed brighter, but the sadness, the fear she had worn when she'd looked at Dray, disappeared and was replaced with a hard smirk. As she raised her fingers again towards his cheek, he knew she would not tenderly feel at what she had always feared was there.

And as her sharp nails pushed into his skin, he closed his arms around her. He breathed out the relief of finally having her in his arms again and cried out at the pain she caused. To hold her small frame against his chest. She cried out from the strong grip.

He squeezed his eyes shut against the world, but it was too late. The white light washed over them, the dragon fire hot, burning at his flesh and very soul. The bright light of Belle blinded him. Even with his eyes closed, he could see nothing but white, could hear nothing but the woman in his arms screaming in pain.

It was the only way to stop them. The only way forward. She had to die, and he would die with her.

# 29

Salima stood over the smouldering remains before turning her attention to the mayhem that continued around them. She had thought that with the death of the queen, they would instantly cease, and she was saddened that they had lost Dray as well, although she had known he wouldn't survive this fight.

Too many had died to end this madness, but it was Ende's death that cut her deepest, despite her knowing full well that it was coming. She had seen him, not just with his face burnt, but falling burning from the sky, despite his being made of fire. But as she had looked over his lifeless body, it had hurt her far more than she had imagined it could.

Papa had watched silently from the other side of the trees. She could feel his hurt, although it was more for her than for the loss of his friend. She looked around now, desperate to find him. She had lost sight of him when they had left the safety of the trees; she had been too busy trying to help weaken them.

The mist slowly began to lift, and Salima realised that the sound wasn't of fighting but confusion at what was happening, which she couldn't quite work out herself. She walked as a woman through the muddy field, the shadows dissipating in the sunshine. Although Belle still shone, there were no longer any screams that followed.

As the mist lifted completely, she stared out over the battlefield. There were more dead than she had thought, but she couldn't determine which side they were on. Many of the bodies were once shadows thought to have been lost, but the shadows had given them up when they died.

She thought one was the regent, but his face was not what it had been, and she wasn't as sure as she would have liked. There were soldiers she recognised from the capital.

"Dray!" a voice called across the field. Salima looked around for the brother she had hoped had survived to find him walking towards her. "Dray!" he called again. He looked across the field and smiled when he saw her.

Salima shook her head slowly, looking back to the charred remains to find they were gone. Perhaps they had dissolved into the earth. He was a man, after all, not like the shadows she had weakened with her fire. But the queen might have been something very different.

"Have you seen Dray?" Ed asked, breathless as he arrived beside her looking down over the ground at their feet.

"It was the only way," Salima whispered.

"What was?"

"He was the only one who could keep her in place."

Papa appeared before her then, looking down as Ed was at the charred ground. "Is she gone?" he asked.

She nodded, and Ed reached for her hand. It wasn't so long ago that he had held it.

"Ende thought Dray might be the only way to reach her in the dark," Papa said.

"Wherever they are now, they are together," Salima whispered. Dray had always known he would die out here, that this was what he was for.

Belle stepped silently forward. She still glowed, although not as brightly, and Salima wondered if she would glow forever now that she had found it.

Ed dropped to his knees, his hands pushing into the blackened earth. Then he lifted out the crown, muddy and tarnished yet reflecting Belle's light. He let out a relieved sob, and Belle helped him to his feet. He stared for too long at the crown in his hand before he threw his arms around her and pulled her close.

"Are they all gone?" Belle asked.

"I think so." Salima looked over the battlefield once more. "Unless she somehow survived and stole them all away."

"There are too many of the shadows destroyed," Papa said. "You weakened, we killed. Many of these dead are just dead, and not by our hands. I don't think they survived the separation. That is what you did, isn't it?" he asked. "You separated her from her magic."

"You separated her from the magic that had awoken in the capital. She always had a magic, although not as powerful," the mage said, appearing in the small group as though he too were made of shadows. "Your Majesty," he said with a bow of his head. "Where do we go from here? Back home?"

"Is it home?" Ed asked. "Ende had called her a mage at one point. Do you think she might have been something different?"

"We'll never know," the mage muttered, heading across the field and, Salima thought, towards the capital.

She didn't want to return to the capital, although she wasn't sure where she did want to go. She wanted to soar free for a time, like she had with Ende once she'd known what was coming. And yet she didn't want to be anywhere without him. She looked back to the trees as the Near Folk stood at the edge of the forest, and she smiled. Then she started to laugh.

"Salima?" Ed asked, looking towards them. "What could possibly be funny?"

She felt the sadness overwhelm her again, the loss and the hurt.

Ed stepped forward and wiped at a tear that had run down her cheek. "There is much to do, but you don't have to come back with us if you don't want to."

"The Near Folk have something for you," she said, throwing her arms around him and holding him tight enough that he groaned.

"Go with them. I will do what I can here, and we shall see each other again."

"Soon?" he asked, trying to hold on to her as she let him go.

"I am always close when you need me, brother."

"I need you now," he said, still holding her tight.

"Go with your friends, and I will find you soon."

Salima watched them go, sending Papa with them, then turned to Barlow and some of the other soldiers. "Go to the capital," she directed. "Ensure it is safe for when the king is ready to return. We might have won here, but I fear they might just be hiding elsewhere."

They bowed, each with fist over heart as they bent low.

"Take the mage with you," she said, watching him walk amongst the dead, poking one occasionally with a foot and then squatting beside another. "Leave the fallen," she commanded. "No matter who they are."

Barlow bowed again and took a group of men with him, stopping to drag the mage away from whatever body he had found. Salima could have guessed at the body he had discovered, but she wanted to believe he was as loyal to Ed as he had claimed to be.

"Collect them together," she told the remaining soldiers, and then she noticed some of the forest men watching from the trees. Another lost, she looked over those around them and found the Lord of Near Forest. He had appeared to be something different from what he had been, and he had become an excellent ally for the king. The Lord of the Grassland stood near, the Lord of the Dry walking towards him, both splattered with blood and mud.

"They can all go together," she said softly, looking at the lord's body. He appeared so much younger than when she had last seen him. But then, she supposed she looked younger than what she had been not so long ago.

"Your Highness," the Lord of the Dry said, bowing her head, and Salima smiled at the idea of it. They too directed their soldiers and men to pull together the dead, both their own and those who had been something else or supported the queen.

Salima stepped back from the group once they were all together. She leapt into the air, became the dragon and, with the fire that had separated the shadows from the men, she burnt the remains of those who had died to ash, leaving nothing but scorched earth. She pulled higher into the sky, out over the forest and the plains, towards the mountains and towards the memory of a man she had never really known.

# 30

Ana opened her eyes to darkness and sucked in a scared breath. It had been dark for so long, but her last memory was of light—blinding, brilliant light. She could still see stars, bright flashes of light as she blinked. Then she was sitting slowly, feeling her body as though she no longer recognised it.

Someone murmured beside her. A strong hand wrapped around hers twitched, squeezed and was followed by a snore.

Ana blinked slowly as her eyes adjusted to the dim light and the stars twinkled above her. She looked over her hand and then at the one still trapped by another. The owner's head was face down with dark shaggy hair. She ran her fingers through it, feeling the texture and wondering if it should be familiar. And then dark brown eyes looked up at her, and the face that lifted from the bed wore an angry red wound across one cheek.

She slapped her hand across her mouth as a large tear ran slowly down his cheek.

"Dray," she whispered hoarsely, her voice not quite her own. "What…" She reached out for his face, sure he would pull away from her, and yet he didn't. He flinched as her fingers brushed over the angry skin, but he didn't move away. He leaned into her hand.

She sobbed with the relief at seeing him, as though it had been so long. She knew it was her fault that he had been injured, that the still-new mark he wore across his check was because of her. He leaned forward, pressed his lips to hers and wrapped his large strong arms around her. He pulled her half from the bed against his chest. All the while he kissed her, hungrily, desperately, and she didn't want to let him go. But she struggled for breath, pushed him away and brushed her thumb over the tears that flowed freely down his cheek.

Ana looked back over hands she wasn't sure were hers. The skin was not quite right, the nails long and black. She didn't feel like she fit into her own body. She wanted to run, not quite sure whether to or from something, but the movement itched beneath her skin.

Dray sat silently watching over her.

"How are we here?" she asked, putting her hand to her throat, sure that she didn't sound herself.

He shrugged, but he never took his eyes from her, and the smile never left his lips.

"How long were you awake?"

"Not long."

"What happened?" she asked again, and he shook his head.

She watched him, wondering what he knew that he wouldn't tell her.

"I only remember the dark," she said, trying not to be overwhelmed. There was too much she didn't understand. She put a hand to her chest, pulling at the thick material. The weight inside her was gone. The magic that had given her strength and promise was no more, and she remembered her desperate fear that it might happen, that they would be separated. She pushed past Dray to stand in the middle of the small space and look around. The stars sparkled above them. She closed her eyes, searching for something, anything. She could feel the ground, feel the earth and the trees, and despite her fears she was calm. Complete.

Dray's strong arms closed around her from behind, but she didn't feel trapped. She felt safe. He had been there in the dark, closing his arms around her, holding her tight so that she couldn't follow the shadows far away. Her heart broke, and a sob escaped.

He turned her slowly, and his brow creased. The fresh slice across his face screamed at her of pain and loss.

"You were prepared to die for me," she gasped. He pulled her against his chest. The strong beat of his heart was steady against her cheek and helped calm her own racing heart.

"I would do anything for you," he whispered across her hair, and she wanted to cry all the more.

"Why? After all that has happened."

"Do you remember what happened?"

She shook her head against his chest, wrapping her arms around him and holding him tight. But she did. In the darkness behind her closed lids, she remembered it all. Much of it as though she were watching someone else's story—and yet she felt the power in her hands, the want for the crown, the desperation to hold on to what was hers. "Is it over?"

"I don't know," he said, his strong arms around her, holding her still and close. In some ways it didn't matter; her part in it was over.

"Was I wearing the crown?" she asked, feeling the loss of the weight.

He took her shoulders and stretched her out before him, and she raised her eyes to his damaged face. Every time she saw it anew, it was like a sharp pain through her chest. "You were," he said.

"Where are we?" she asked, looking around, but she knew. She could feel it. They were in the trees, in the forest, protected from the darkness. "Can she return?"

"Who?" he asked, his dark eyes focused on her as though she might disappear if he looked away.

"Me," she whispered, hoping her voice didn't crack again.

"Ana, she was never you."

"She was. We were born together, connected more than I can explain, and yet she wasn't always there."

"The light," he said, trying to hold on to her, but she pulled out of his reach. She needed to think, work out just what she had done and how she might undo it. "Belle's light and the dragon's fire burned away the shadows."

"You can't kill a shadow—it isn't that easy," she snapped.

He looked down then, and she wondered at his sword, where it might be, why he didn't have it with him.

"Ende," she whispered, her voice catching again in her throat. After all he had done to help her find herself, although she had become something very different from what she wanted to be and just what he had feared. She allowed Dray to take her in his arms again. "Why are we here? How could they allow me into the trees?"

He shook his head, his rough chin rubbing against the top of her head.

"You have always saved me," she whispered, wanting to stay in his arms forever. She closed her eyes and leaned into him, thinking of the first day they had met, his strong hand around her arm, his smile when she'd worn his cloak, his carrying her across the bridge. "I don't deserve your friendship."

"You have it anyway." She could hear the smile in his voice. "And you have saved me often enough."

"Hardly," she murmured.

"There was a soldier prepared to run me through in my sleep."

"You could have taken him," she said. Although she knew full well she had taken the man before Dray had the chance. "Does he hate me?" she asked. "Ed."

"Never."

She huffed. "You are a good friend."

"Ana," he said carefully, holding her out again, but she couldn't look up at him.

"Sit down," she said, her voice strong and commanding. He backed up and did just that, although he held her hand and pulled her toward the bed. As he lifted his face to her, she saw something very different, something she had never thought he would show her, and she gulped down the growing fear in her chest. She slowly lifted her hand and touched her fingers to the bloody slash across his face that she had seen so many times before it was there. He closed his eyes and squeezed her hand tighter in his.

Ana took a deep breath and felt the forest move around her, felt the solidness of the ground beneath her feet. She brushed her fingers over it again and again.

"It burns," he whispered, but he didn't move, didn't flinch. He kept his face turned up to her.

She leant forward, eyes closed, and pressed her lips to the thin line as she breathed in the scent of his skin. He released her hand and wrapped his arms around her, holding her close. She breathed out the calm solid earth that filled her being across his skin. Her hands moved to cup his face, and her lips brushed his. Before she leaned back and staggered a little, he held her easily. His fingers moved to his cheek, where a faint white line was all that remained.

"You have magic," he whispered, but he didn't show the fear she thought he would. Didn't flinch away from her or loosen his grip.

"It is the magic of the earth, of the trees, of the air," a voice that sounded like the wind said behind her. She turned as Dray climbed slowly to his feet, his hand finding hers and holding tight. "It is a magic you have always had, one exploited by another."

Ana took in the older man, the chief of the Near Folk. "You did this," she said.

"We allowed for it to happen, but it was you who did this."

She shook her head.

"The light caused the separation you needed and, conscious or not of what you were, your magic kept him safe." He looked over her at the tall man behind her. "It brought you both to where you were safe."

"I can move through the shadows?" The fear was overwhelming as she stepped forward. She wasn't any different. "You have to kill me now," she said, turning to Dray. For the first time she saw uncertainty, but he shook his head.

"There will always be shadows," the chief said, and she turned back to him. "They can no longer reach you. They can no longer cause the pain they did."

Ana thought her heart would explode. Dray's hand, still in hers, held her tight. She closed her eyes and breathed in the smell of the earth.

"It is time for you to go home," he said. "Your friends come."

"I can't," she murmured, turning to Dray. "I can't see them."

"Of course you can," he said, striding past her and dragging her out into the early morning light of the trees.

Ed could have lain down for a week, he was so exhausted. He was covered in blood and mud, and the crown still hung from his fingers. People had bowed to him as he had left the field and headed into the trees, and he wondered what the Near Folk had in store. Although the look on Salima's face had told him it was good news, he still doubted. The chief had walked from the cottage, Dray not far behind him, and Ed had never felt so relieved in all his life.

"Dray," he called, rushing forward, then stopped as Dray turned to him and a woman stepped from the darkened doorway behind him. Ana.

His first response was to turn and flee, but his legs didn't appear to feel the same, for they wouldn't move at all. She looked at him, her eyes scared. She tried to hold Dray back, but he continued towards him, and Ed clung tighter to the crown in his hand.

Dray released the woman and clamped both hands down on Ed's shoulders. "I am pleased to see you," he said, and Ed realised he had never seen him smile in such a way in all the time had known him.

Ed nodded, unsure of what he could say. He glanced past the

large man at the woman who appeared even smaller standing on her own, her hands clenched before her, her eyes on the ground.

"Ana!" Belle broke the silence, stepping forward as Dray prevented Ed from holding her back. Then she wrapped her arms around Ana. Ed thought she might have glowed a little, but he wasn't sure, and as she pulled Ana close, she crumpled into her. "We have you now," she said.

Dray dropped his hold as Ed stepped forward and, without raising her eyes, Ana curtsied before him. He released the breath he had been holding and did as Belle had, wrapping his arms around her, feeling her shiver in his hold. He held her closer.

"I thought you were dead," he stammered. "Both of you."

"Ana," Dray said, as though by way of explanation.

"It may have been you too," Belle said. Ana sniffed and lifted her head. "I've seen something in him." Ana looked at Dray then as though for the first time. Ed released his hold and watched her step up to him. Ed had never seen the man smile so much; it was as though he had been bewitched. She put her hand on his arm and closed her eyes, then walked slowly around him, looking to the ground.

She looked back at Belle and shook her head.

"I feel it," Belle reassured her.

"The chief thinks it is Ana's magic that protected us in the end and brought us here."

"Maybe," Belle said. And then she stepped forward and threw her arms around Dray, pulling him close.

Ana looked up then, and Ed saw her green eyes as they had always been, bright but not glowing.

"Your face," he said quickly, noticing the fine white line.

Dray's fingers moved to his cheek.

Ed looked around the group and noticed Forest standing back. Ana took a deep breath and then stepped up to him and took his hands. "I'm sorry," she said, and he nodded once. "Where is she?"

"Not where I left her," he said, but his smile was sad. Ed

wondered what Salima had done. She had sent them on ahead, and in that moment he realised she wouldn't be following. Not for some time.

Ana turned back to the group and gave a small smile as Dray beamed at her. "I need to go home," she said.

"We will leave as soon as you are ready," Ed said.

She shook her head. "Sheer Rock, Your Majesty. I need to return to Sheer Rock."

Ed didn't want to lose her again. And as he reached for her, her hands rested on the crown in his hand. What had not so long ago been hard black rock was bright shiny silver. He let her take it, and she smiled a genuine smile as she raised it up and placed it on his head. Her eyes sparkled, and a tear ran quickly down one cheek.

"I'm sorry," she whispered, "that it took me so long to find your crown." Her hands hovered on the metal and then his face, and she stretched up on her toes to kiss his cheek. "Forgive me, Your Majesty."

He pulled her close, and she wrapped her arms around him and squeezed him tight. He cried out. She stepped back and then looked down at her hands. They were covered in blood, and she screamed.

It was Dray who silenced her, pulling her in tight against his chest, her clenched fists held out to the side as though too afraid to hold anything. Ed had thought he'd caught a blade at some point during the fight, but he had carried on despite the stinging. It was Belle who stepped forward and pulled at his jerkin, then at his shirt.

"Ana," she said. "Ana!" she repeated. The other woman turned, peering over Dray's arm. "I need your help."

"It isn't so bad," Ed murmured, then sucked in a breath as she poked him. "I think you took a little too much enjoyment from that. It happened early; it isn't so bad."

"It might become bad. You appear to have lost more blood than you know. More than I realised."

Master Forest had moved closer again. "We might need to stitch it."

"I am not having you work on me like a dress."

Belle had motioned Ana forward again, and she peered carefully around his back as though the wound might harm her.

"I didn't do this," she murmured.

"No," he said kindly.

She pressed her hand to his back, and he grunted as she released the pressure. Belle pressed her hand over hers. Ed struggled to watch them both over his shoulder, but Ana sucked in a deep breath and they stared at each other before they both closed their eyes. His skin itched and tingled, and he looked up to find the smile had slipped from Dray's face.

"You can't feel responsible for everything," Ed said.

"Shh," Belle murmured.

Ana's other hand had snaked around to the front, where it held tight to his shirt.

"Where will you go?" Ed asked Dray, trying to ignore the women pressed against him.

"Home," he said. Ana turned then and stepped away from him.

"With us?" Ed asked, but Dray shook his head, his eyes on Ana.

"Home is where Ana is," he said, the small smile returning. She let out a long breath, as though she had been holding it, and she was back in his arms.

"Where is your armour?" Ed asked, unsure what else to say.

"I've left it behind," he said, looking down at the woman in his arms.

"I knew you had magic," Belle whispered.

# 31

Ed tried to look like he felt comfortable on the throne. And despite all the work to get there, he felt it wasn't his place. And then a hand closed around his on the smooth carved armrest and he breathed out slowly as he turned to the woman beside him.

On a matching throne beside his, close enough that they could reach each other, sat his wife. She was just as beautiful as she had always been. And although she didn't quite shine like she had, when she smiled it lit up the world around her.

"Your Majesty," Sword Master Forest said, bowing low and smiling broadly. "The armour has been melted down, the old armour of the King's Men reinstated and there are many keen to sign up."

Ed nodded slowly. "I leave it with you to select the best of men."

Forest bowed low again and then stepped back. Ed had offered him whatever title or position he wanted, but he only wanted to return to the practice halls and training the young men of the kingdom. Ed was happy enough to allow that to happen. He only hoped it wasn't too long before his sister returned to visit with them both. Although he knew it wouldn't be any time soon.

Despite his discomfort he had slipped easily enough into giving orders and advice, and to take it from others. People were still wary of visiting the throne room, and there were those who had been gifted positions not so long ago from a queen wanting much in return. He still had a lot to prove to the people.

There were still whispers of him in the hallways as the boy king. But it wasn't malicious, more a term of endearment and he was trying to accept it for what it was.

"There is something I want to show you," Belle whispered.

"Will I like it?"

"Of course." She grinned as she stood and held out her hand to him.

He took it and allowed her to lead the way, two soldiers followed behind and they were already aware of what spaces they could and couldn't follow him into. He had spent much time reacquainting himself with a castle he had barely seen since he was a child. It was larger and more overwhelming than he remembered, and yet he found happy memories in most rooms and corners that had helped him settle in.

They moved towards the tower and the royal suite, somewhere he had once been very comfortable, but his memories had been clouded by his uncle. Despite all his new wife did to try and convince him, they were staying in his small room, near the servants. They were headed up the stairs when he stopped.

"That is new," he said.

"Is it?" But she wore a grin, one that told him she was up to something.

He pushed into the room to find a room he had never seen before, the windows melted, part of the wall, burnt and tumbled down. "Ende?"

"And Salima. This was where she moved me to."

He turned from the view to Belle, wondering what she was thinking.

"It was such a strange room," she continued, releasing his hand and stepping forward. "I can't find anything in the library that tells me how or when it was created. But there was no door. A room completely sealed away."

He turned back to the door. And then looked up. So close to the royal suite and he wondered who else over the centuries had magic to gain entrance into a sealed room. And why they would need such a space.

"It is small, but light and comfortable. I thought it might make a nice retreat."

It did feel comfortable, like his old room was familiar and he nodded. "The fresh air is nice."

She smiled then. "It is to be fixed. I have something else to show you," she said, heading back out to the stairs and holding out her hand for him.

"Is it missing walls?"

"One," she said, pulling him along. The soldiers had remained at the base of the stairs and he was thankful for the time. There seemed to be so little he had with her alone.

His heart pounded in his chest so loudly he was sure she could hear it as he stepped into the royal suite that had once, so long ago, been his childhood home. He had imagined his uncle here and then Ana when she wasn't herself, and yet it was so different, he couldn't get a sense of either of them.

Several large soft chairs filled the space directly in front of him, a small table between them, and then along from them, a long table with bench seats running along both sides. A simple candelabra sat in the middle. Across from the table was the balcony his father had stood at so often, looking out over the city.

At the far end of the room a large map, painted on the wall depicted the Kingdom of Ilia, from the Dry in the far south, to the islands of Sheer Rock in the far north. He ran his fingers over it as he stepped out onto the balcony. The sun reflected from windows beneath him, people moved along the streets, the sound of people getting on with their lives travelled up to him, and he remembered that day looking at market stalls.

As he turned back to Belle, standing in the middle of the room, her hands held too tight before her he smiled, and his hand ran over the railing and he stopped and looked back. The stone was cracked through, although it was still strong and the balustrade held together.

"Ana," Belle whispered, coming up to stand beside him. "We can have it replaced."

He shook his head slowly, running his finger through the gap in the stone. "It is good to be reminded of what went before."

"There is more," she said, putting her hand to his arm, and indicated a door behind her.

He sighed, but nodded and she opened the door, standing back to let him enter first.

It was bright with a large window filling the room with sunlight. He stopped and looked over the empty space. Then back to Belle, who smiled. The only furniture in the room, was a narrow mattress in the middle of the floor. It reminded him of their time in an attic in the city below, when he thought Ana was helping, but it seemed out of place in the large space.

Belle closed the door and moved to the mattress, where she sat gracefully in the middle of it. "I thought we should rethink the furniture in here. And I didn't want to sleep in a bed someone else had been in."

"And this was the option."

"I have something grand coming," she said, looking around the room as he sat down beside her. "Something fit for a king."

"This would do."

"Really? I remember something like this before," she whispered, leaning forward. "You don't need curtains?"

"We have a whole floor of a castle and soldiers ensuring no one disturbs us." He leant forward and kissed her gently.

"Won't they miss the king?" she asked, pulling back.

"Not just yet," he said, capturing her in his arms and pulling her close. "Let's give it a couple of days and see what happens." He kissed down her neck as she giggled, she glowed brightly, but that might have been the sunshine behind her.

＊

Dray watched Ana stop at the edge of the bridge. She had become increasingly nervous as they approached the northern end of the kingdom, but she had smiled at him every time he looked at her. As he joined her at the bridge, he noted the lack of soldiers and wondered just what had happened here during the last few months.

She took his hand and walked out onto the bridge without a word. He matched her step for step, not too fast and not racing. When they reached the other end, there were no soldiers there either.

"We have more to go," he said.

"I'm not afraid," she said, looking up at him.

"Of the bridge?"

She nodded slowly and gave him a sad smile. "I'm not sure when it happened, but I'm not afraid anymore."

He didn't know what to say. The first thing that came to mind was, "Do you want to go home first, or the castle?"

"Why isn't there anyone here?" she asked.

"I don't know," he said, wondering just what they might find. There was still a walk to the castle he could see in the distance, and he rested his hand on his sword.

"I'm glad you found it," she said, giving his hand a little squeeze.

"Belle had a good idea of where it was."

Ana nodded and looked ahead.

"Ana?" he asked.

She shook her head as though not wanting to answer whatever question he might have formed. When they had said goodbye, she had held Belle for a long time before releasing her. They had waved them off to the south while heading north. The king had insisted they take the horses, but Ana wanted to feel the earth beneath her feet, and Dray was in no rush for them to join others.

"I wonder where Salima is?" he asked as they passed the quiet houses. Ana stopped. He looked down to find her looking at one of the cottages, and she sighed before heading to it.

"She was in the mountains," Ana said after a little while, opening the door of the house without knocking.

"I didn't see her. Did you?"

"She was there," Ana said, smiling up at him. The man at the table stood quickly, pushing the chair back, and Dray's hand was on his sword again.

"Ana?" the man asked as she stepped forward and threw her arms around him. "Where have you been? You headed off on an errand and never returned. The mage nearly turned the islands over looking for you."

"Where is the mage?" Dray asked.

"He returned to the capital to help, but Belle will watch him."

"Ana!" the man said. She released him and stepped back.

"Tom, thank you for watching over the house."

"I thought you would return one day," he said, running his hands through his hair, and Dray saw the boy who had stopped them to check she had her cloak. She still didn't, although she had assured him she didn't need one. She was at least dressed in lighter colours, although the dark had suited her.

"Is he to stay?" Tom asked, indicating Dray with a chin.

"We have to go to the castle," Ana said, heading back to the door.

"She's gone," he said, his hands fidgeting as he looked between them. "The queen turned her into something else, and then she was dead. There were others too. We weren't sure what they were, but we didn't know if the queen was coming for them or not and so we burnt them."

Ana nodded slowly, looking down at the floor before she took a deep breath and turned back to Dray.

"She's gone, the queen, isn't she?" Tom asked, fear evident on his voice. "We might have been far away, but she could reach anywhere at any time."

"She's gone," Dray reassured him, and Ana turned and left the cottage.

"Did she do something to Ana?"

Dray shook his head and followed her out.

"I don't know that I can be here," she whispered as he came up beside her.

"Let's go to the castle."

She nodded once and led the way towards the next bridge. They continued in silence until halfway over it, where she stopped and walked towards the edge. Something like fear caught in Dray's throat as he watched her. He reached for her when she turned and smiled up at him.

"I thought my father had fallen from a bridge," she said, looking out into the gap between the islands. "As a child, the height never frightened me, and then when he was gone, I couldn't bear it."

Dray stepped up beside her and looked out over the edge himself. He was reminded of the Walk.

"It wasn't until I was on the Walk that I remembered what had happened, that I had been there with him that day and my aunt had dragged me back into the room, although I'll never know why. That was the fear."

"I can understand it," Dray said, stepping back from the edge. "I'm not keen myself now."

"She took my fears away, all of them. Some returned, but not that one."

"Who?" he asked, but he wasn't sure he wanted to hear the answer.

"The queen," she murmured. "I remember what I did. I remember how I felt. When I came to visit my aunt, I was angry, hurt. I wanted her to bow down to me. I wanted her to know what I was."

She looked around at him, her bright eyes sparkling with unshed tears. "She was mine in the end," she said, turning back to the view. "I guess I knew they would die when I did."

They continued in silence towards the castle, hand in hand, and when they crossed the last bridge, the soldier who had been so rude last time they had passed this way bowed politely and silently to Ana. Dray wondered if he recognised her, but when he looked back over his shoulder, the man was watching them walk on.

Instead of the front door of the castle, Ana walked towards the servant's entrance. She pushed open the heavy door, and Dray followed her through the dark corridors. Then she stopped in a doorway. The smell of fresh bread filled his senses and made his mouth water. Ana waited, watching the plump woman work at the table. When she looked up, she beamed and raced forward, throwing her arms around Ana and nearly pushing Dray down in the process.

"My child," she murmured, squeezing her tight.

"Can't breathe," Ana called.

"You have stayed away too long," the woman chastised. "But I am glad you are home. Go up now, and I'll send someone with tea and bread." She waved at Ana, who shook her head and sat down at the large table.

"You can't sit here, not now."

"You just called me *child*," Ana said, a confidence returning that Dray hadn't heard enough. "I will sit where I choose."

"Then the gentleman had better sit with you. Are you hungry, sir?"

Ana laughed as Dray scooted her along the bench and sat beside her.

The cook turned and put her hands on her ample waist. He was reminded briefly of Ana doing something similar, but she had been only a girl then. He put his hand on hers.

"He's a soldier," she said.

"I can be whatever you need me to be," Dray responded.

"You'll always be my soldier," Ana whispered, and the cook

grinned at them.

"Well, whatever it is you think you are, you are the lord now and should be sitting upstairs like lords do."

Ana put her other hand over Dray's as though he might take it away. "I plan to be a different sort of lord," she said.

"Ah, one that gets under my feet. Back to how we were then, lass."

Ana smiled, still looking down at Dray's hand, but it was the most genuine smile he had seen for some time. On a whim, he leant forward and kissed her temple, only because it was closest.

"Well, ain't no lord been doing that in the kitchen before," the cook said. "Let's get you fed and then settled, my lady."

Ana opened her mouth to protest, but Dray shook his head as the cook turned away. She gave him a single nod.

"You'll have to learn to behave when the king comes to visit," Dray whispered.

"You know the king?" the cook asked, pouring tea into cups for them. Dray watched as she sliced large chunks from a hot loaf of bread.

"Ana put the crown on his head," he said, distracted by the bread.

"I worried for you out there all alone. When we heard of the witch queen, we didn't know what might have happened. When your mother was lost in the capital so long ago, I feared the same."

Dray could see the hurt as Ana sipped her tea.

"They don't seem to know it was me," Ana said, standing at the opening to the Walk, allowing the wind to pull at her dress and hair. It smelt different, felt different, and she no longer feared it. But as she made to step out onto the platform, a strong hand closed around her arm and pulled her back.

"You might not be scared," Dray rumbled, holding her close,

"but I am. And it wasn't you," he added softly. His breath was like another breeze across her skin, and it was as though she could feel the entire world around her. His lips pressed against her forehead, his rough beard brushing against her skin as she leaned into him.

"You smell like bread," she whispered.

"Mmm," he murmured, still holding her close. "I could live on that bread."

"I'm sure we can be fed more than just bread and tea."

"I'd be happy," he said, kissing her neck.

"Dray," she said, stepping back.

"I'm not leaving," he said too quickly.

"I don't want you to leave," she said, her heart beating too fast. She looked around the large room, cold and open and with very little in it. "I hate this room," she said.

"You can make it yours." He stood back and indicated the room with a sweep of his hand.

She closed her eyes and breathed out slowly, trying to imagine what would make the room more comfortable. There was a whole grey castle wrapped around it, and she thought of the castle in the mountains. But the grey stone belonged to the coast, to the islands. She imagined the cliff faces and the small plants that grew amongst their crevices.

When she opened her eyes, it was as though she had awoken in a different world. She could smell the sea and the earth and the trees. Ferns and orchids grew amongst the stones of the wall. A blanket of soft green grass stretched across what had been hard stone floor. She turned slowly, taking in the wonder of it. Dray stood amongst it, grinning like a child.

The only thing not changed was the Walk. The hard, squared stone reached out over the sea. Small climbing plants had claimed the opening. She ran her hand through the soft leaves as she stepped out, allowing the wind that smelt of salt to pull at her. In the distance, out over the water, as the sky turned orange, Ana was certain a dragon soared like a bird on the currents.

ACKNOWLEDGMENTS

The team at Deranged Doctor Designs (DDD) for absolutely brilliant cover design work and all the marketing extras. Thank you for your support and clear emails around what is needed from me to make the magic happen.

TWG members, and Melissa, for listening and support in all things writing related. Special thanks to Yasmin for taking the time to read my draft and providing ideas to make the story stronger.

Allison E Wright for wonderful editing work to make my sentences smoother and my intentions clearer.

My parents, Francine and Ken Smith. Amazing, supportive people who I don't thank often enough. Thanks for keeping me grounded and being the best grandparents ever.

As always, Temwa for being my biggest supporter.

# ABOUT THE AUTHOR

Georgina Makalani survives life as a servant of the public by hiding in her office at lunch time with dragons, witches, a laptop and a little bit of magic.

For more about Georgina and her books visit her website: www.theflowofink.com